The DISCOVERY *of* DAWN

First published in the United States of America in 2008
by Rizzoli Ex Libris, an imprint of
Rizzoli International Publications, Inc.
300 Park Avenue South
New York, NY 10010
www.rizzoliusa.com

© 2008 Walter Veltroni
Translated by Douglas Hofstadter

Original Title: LA SCOPERTA DELL'ALBA
© 2006 RCS Libri S.p.A., Milan

2008 2009 2010 2011 / 10 9 8 7 6 5 4 3 2 1

Printed in the United States
ISBN-13: 978-0-8478-3109-8
Library of Congress Control Number: 2008925833

The DISCOVERY *of* DAWN

WALTER VELTRONI

Rizzoli
ex libris

When, in October of 2006, I received an unexpected email invitation to be a speaker in the first-ever *Festival della Matematica* in Rome the following March, I had mixed feelings about flying all the way across the Atlantic for just a few days. Why do such a crazy thing? I might well have declined had the list of invitees not been absolutely star-studded: Andrew ("Fermat's Last Theorem") Wiles, John (*A Beautiful Mind*) Nash, Benoit ("Mr. Fractals") Mandelbrot, Michael Atiyah and Alain Connes (Fields Medal winners), Dario Fo and Zhores Alferov (Nobel Prize winners in literature and physics), and last but not least, Boris Spassky, former world chess champion and Bobby Fischer's opponent in the unforgettable USA/USSR chess showdown in Reykjavik in 1972. But what really intrigued me was that this invitation had been issued by Walter Veltroni, Mayor of Rome. Why on earth was Rome's mayor organizing a mathematics festival, of all things? I had no idea, but as a lifelong lover of mathematics, I thought it was admirable and quite extraordinary.

The previous summer, my daughter Monica, then just four-teen, had spent a few days in Rome with an Italian friend, and the entire time Monica heard nonstop praise for the Eternal City's mayor from everyone she met. Romans of all political stripes admired him for his ideas, his generosity, and his progressiveness. By the time she left Rome, Monica was wild about its mayor. And so when I received this dazzling invitation just a few months later, I instantly went to Monica's bedroom and read it aloud to her. Not surprisingly, she burst out, "We *have* to go!" And that was that—or *nearly* that.

To make it *fully* that, I wrote back to the person from whom the email had come—my friend Piergiorgio Odifreddi, a well-known Italian mathematician and author, who was organizing the festival for Veltroni—and said, "I'd love to come with my two kids, but do you think the mayor would show up and at least shake our hands? My daughter would be thrilled." The next day Piergiorgio wrote back, saying that Mayor Veltroni not only would gladly meet us but in fact would very much like us to come visit him in his office on the Campidoglio (one of Rome's seven famous hills) where, from a high balcony, he would share his magnificent view of the Roman Forum with us. Well now, that was *really* that.

In March of 2007, my children Danny and Monica flew with me from Indianapolis to Rome. We were treated like VIPs the whole time we were there—a beautiful week of balmy spring weather. As advertised, the Math Festival was an amazing event, and we indeed met all the celebrities—in fact, we all chatted for hours together during several dinners. This was a thrill! But what Danny, Monica, and I anticipated the most was the promised visit with Mayor Veltroni—and he came through for us in flying colors.

Bright and early on Friday, March 16—by coincidence Danny's nineteenth birthday—we were driven from our fancy hotel to the heart of Rome. We walked up Capitoline Hill and admired the splendid piazza designed by Michelangelo. Once inside the City Hall, we were soon ushered into the mayor's spacious if slightly cluttered office.

Mayor Veltroni greeted us warmly, offering us delicious coffee, tea, and pastries, and then we began chatting in a jolly, informal fashion. He asked why we all spoke Italian, and I explained that since our family had spent three years in Italy, we always speak Italian at home in order not to lose the language. Then he asked Danny about his prospective major in college, and Monica about her main interests. "Fashion," she replied, upon which she presented him with a lovely yellow scarf and hat adorned with maroon pom-poms (the colors of the Rome soccer team), which she'd knitted for him in Bloomington. Being an avid sports fan, the mayor couldn't have been more touched. Then he told us about his political idols—great figures such as Nelson Mandela, Mahatma Gandhi, and Robert Kennedy. This last name touched me deeply, since I'd been an ardent RFK supporter until his tragic assassination, the shock of which had propelled me into years of political activism. I thus felt an immediate bond with Walter Veltroni.

Then the mayor swung open the balcony doors and with lively gestures gave us a guided tour of the Roman Forum. At one point, he looked straight down and I saw that, some sixty feet below, a trinket seller was opening up his stand. Veltroni waved down and cried out "Buongiorno!", which was echoed by a wave, a smile, and an upwards-floating "Buongiorno!" I deduced that this sweet little exchange between the two men was a daily ritual.

When the mayor heard that my wife Carol had died in Verona when our children were just five and two, he expressed profound sympathy and explained that he, too, had lost his father, when he was just one year old, and that the loss had marked him for life. But he added that, over the years, he had arrived at the personal philosophy that a gaping hole in one's soul can gradually metamorphose into a source of strength, rather than remaining a perpetual cause of sadness. This remark struck me as a deep insight into grappling with tragedy.

After a while, the mayor walked over to a desk and picked up several items, which he proceeded to distribute. To Danny he gave a copy of Antoine de Saint-Exupéry's *Little Prince* (in Italian) and a video about his political philosophy. To Monica he gave the same video and a book he himself had written—his first novel, *La Scoperta dell'Alba* (*The Discovery of Dawn*). Only then did we realize that this thoughtful politician was also an accomplished writer. He gave a copy of his novel to me as well, and signed each item.

We warmly thanked Mayor Veltroni for his kindness and started moving toward the door, but he was in no hurry; indeed, he insisted we contact him the next time we were in Rome, and wrote his personal address on a business card. At last, he graciously ushered us out into the hallway while describing the art on the walls. When finally we emerged into the Roman morning, we all felt our visit had been even more rewarding than anticipated, and I had no doubt that it would forever glow in my children's memories.

On our flight back to Indianapolis, I read *La Scoperta dell'Alba* with avid curiosity. What would a novel penned by the mayor of one of the world's greatest cities be like? I was surprised to find it had elements of South American magical realism, and was touched to see the theme of the loss of a father echoed throughout the book.

I respected Mayor Veltroni so much that, once home, I sent him a letter offering to translate his novel into English. He replied quickly, expressing delight at my offer, and put me in touch with his Italian publisher. And that's how this translation came about.

Over the following months, I greatly enjoyed rendering Veltroni's supple Italian prose into English. As with any type of translation, there were innumerable tricky challenges, of which I'll mention only one here: Veltroni's habit of using sentence fragments instead of full sentences. Sometimes noun phrases. Sometimes adverbs. Adjectives, too. A lot. A strong stylistic hallmark. But one that I instinctively felt wouldn't go down so well in English. And so, after I'd translated two chapters, I sent them to the mayor with a cover letter asking whether it would be all right if I occasionally turned fragments into full sentences, thus slightly altering his prose's tone.

Soon I received a candid reply from Mayor Veltroni, saying that, unfortunately, he didn't speak English well enough to make such decisions, so he'd simply leave it all up to me. As a consequence, I tried to find a happy medium between a literal-minded but timid style of leaving sentence fragments as such and a liberal-spirited but brazen style of always converting fragments into full flowing sentences. This is just one tiny example of the countless subjective judgments that permeated the translation of this novel. Of course, that's par for the course, since translation is a subtle art, not a frozen set of recipes.

A few months after our Roman trip, we heard that Mayor Veltroni had been elected head of the newly founded Partito Democratico and that he would soon oppose the media mogul Silvio Berlusconi in a national election for prime minister. We were naturally excited at the prospect of our new friend becoming Italy's next leader, and watched the news carefully. In February 2008, Mayor Veltroni dramatically resigned from the mayoralty in order to conduct a serious campaign for prime minister. Troublingly, the polls showed him trailing Berlusconi, but this also evoked great respect, as it underlined how great the risk was that he'd taken. To our family's disappointment and that of millions of Italians, Veltroni lost a close election in April to Berlusconi, and thus found himself neither mayor of Rome nor prime minister of Italy.

Who knows what the future will bring for Walter Veltroni. Will he run again for prime minister? Will he try to reform the eternal mess of Italian politics by reducing the number of major parties to just two, on the American model? Or will he instead exploit this fallow period to write more novels? If so, I will be among his most enthusiastic readers.

—Douglas Hofstadter

CHAPTER ONE

It's a rather plain dawn, today. Ever since my biological clock started regularly waking up at daybreak, I've been charting the various types of dawns. I began to notice the special features of the dawns of each of the four seasons, picking out color combinations and positions of the sun, and deciding on my favorites. Every dawn has a meaning, a unique one. And a certain degree of intimate subtlety. But dawn has no dignity. Neither encyclopedias nor Google give it the time of day. It's seen as merely a way to make time pass—an invisible and fleeting wayfarer. And yet that's not what dawn truly is. The dawns I've watched this past year, day after day, are anticipations of God. They comprise silence and grandeur, tradition and change, pausing and waiting, beginning and ending. I watch each one as if it were a world of possibilities—soft, intense, and brimming with colors. But here, up in this attic where I seek refuge the moment I wake up, we're not alone, the dawn and I. We have several companions: the breathing of my wife, who's asleep in the adjoining room, the rhythmic grinding of my daughter Stella's teeth, and distant strains of music drifting out of the earphones of the iPod that my son didn't think of turning off before he fell asleep. And thus, seeking an escape, I turn on the television but leave it on mute, so that colors flicker across the room. And every so often I shift my gaze. And once in a while, in the coolness of morning, I feel I can experience, for just a few moments, the full meaning of life. The marvelous possibility of the dawn, with its colors that announce, foretell, and deceive. The gentle hint of a period of hope. And then those flickering colors, loud as a scream. I can do without the words from the TV, which, in any case, is silent. I see a bloody red and a swath of other colors coming from the burnt-out shells of car bombs. I see the blue-turned-gray of the sea that is nothing but a wave, a huge wave. I see a vulgar shade of light blue, the short skirts of dancers who aren't dancing.

Which of these is reality? Is the real what comes first, like the dawn, or is it what comes later, like television? This is a difficult season for me, because dawn and sunset, hope and disappointment, are fused together. Because my time is dwindling, and as I look back over my life, it seems a decent one but a humble one. It seems as if my own dawn and the world lit up by it should have gotten more from someone like me.

For many years, at the National Archives, my job has been to collect, catalogue, read, and summarize the diaries that my peers never cease producing. Little books, often printed at their authors' expense, in which each person, having come to a certain stage in life, feels a need to tell the world about their existence, and thereby to make it eternal. To make it great, thanks to paper, which, resisting the passage of time, turns this life into a unique one—not a list of forgettable days, but a sequence of close-packed events. Perhaps true, perhaps false, perhaps merely tricks of memory, yet just as strong as genuine memories. Inventions of the will, yearnings for what one might have done, presented as what one did. There are stories of small acts of heroism, of shattered hopes, of dreams pursued in vain. There are stories of wives and comrades, of children and supervisors, of friends who died, always too soon, of loyal pets and of earthshaking photographs. All these are little stories in the greater story. And that's what I liked about this job, when I started—the chance to live many lives. True lives, not imaginary ones like those in novels. I've read thousands of diaries, known thousands of people, felt their pains and joys. I've been father, son, war comrade, benchmate, train traveler, circus performer, mechanic, athlete, and martyr. I've lived thousands of lives, in search of my own. In the pages I've read in my office while listening to piano music, very soft piano music, I've also sought comfort and answers. I've sought the forerunners of my life, sought to live the dawns in reverse order. In those thousands of small, unpretentious books arranged by historical period, by theme, and by geographical area, I have found pages that could speak to me and guide me through my troubles when the world was trembling and I had nothing else to grasp on to.

In the diary of a mother, classified under the label "Hardships," there is a painful recounting of the exact day on which her life trembled and her certainties were reduced to rubble. In the words of that woman both so unknown and so close to me I have sought answers concerning my own earthquake. This woman gave birth to a child in the mid-1960s. She had expected his birth to endow her life with genuine and deep meaning, to make her feel that now she was living and not just drifting aimlessly through time. But there was something wrong with Andrea, her son. The doctors tried hard to squelch the smile on her lips, tried to get her to understand that he was not going to have the life she had imagined for those nine long months, and even earlier, and was still imagining. It was called Down's syndrome, and perhaps it is more of an affliction than an illness. In her diary, the mother related, for many pages on end, the story of her special love for Andrea. She described with great sincerity the rage and the sadness, the humiliations and the anguish that she suffered in parks, in children's games, at school in sports. Andrea was treated badly by innocent children, his peers. They ran away from him, didn't understand him, and he felt more and more isolated. As he grew, he became ever sweeter and more melancholy. He never left the house alone.

One summer afternoon when he was around fourteen, Andrea waited until his parents were napping. He tiptoed toward the door and closed it behind him, feeling as if he owned the world. After pushing the button for the elevator, he crouched down so that no one could see him and tell his mother. He walked out the door of his building and headed for the park. Now joyous and free, he greeted everyone he met on the street. He turned toward the municipal gardens, threading his way between buildings, watching his peers play ball, rooting for one side or the other, choosing at random. He bought himself a chocolate cream and sat down on a bench. The sun was setting and he felt euphoric as he waited, though he didn't know what he was waiting for—or perhaps he did. Far off somewhere, he noticed a patchwork of colors running toward him. He didn't hear the shouts emanating from that wide-open mouth that now he saw and recognized as familiar. His attention was instead focused on the sound of the water in the little fountain near him. He looked at it and smiled and felt grown-up, and the master of his own sounds.

Stella, my Stella—I don't know when she will ever become the master of her own sounds. I do know that now that she's turned twelve, she seems to me to be the very hub of the world.

I feel she is human life distilled into its purest essence. She's generous and she loves her neighbor. She'll hug anyone, neither imagining nor understanding that one person might ever hurt another. That would strike her as senseless, useless, a waste of time.

When Stella was born, my wife was forty years old, and, as I discovered later, the chance of having a child with Down's syndrome goes way up for mothers of that age. The probability for a woman younger than twenty-five is 1 in 1,376, while for a woman of forty it's 1 in 126. That pregnancy was something the two of us had desired and sought. It seemed like a way of bringing back smiles and hopes, a way for us to wake up in the morning together and to dream about the future. Also, we thought that Lorenzo would be happy to have a little brother or sister, now that he was eight. This was our last chance to have children who would forge a tight bond.

But when they carried Stella in to Giulia to be nursed for the first time, I saw a strange look come over Giulia's face. The smile that accompanied her hands as they softly caressed the baby's nose, ears, and tummy was not serene and untroubled. As I went back and forth between hospital and home, I didn't notice the slightest difference between what I saw on Stella's face and the faces of the other little wiggling babies in the nursery. But what do I know? I'm just a father. One morning I entered Giulia's room in the maternity ward and found her sobbing, face pressed into her pillow. She stopped her crying and looked up at me with teary eyes. We remained wordless for a few moments, fearful of speaking to each other. Then she quietly said to me, "Stella has Down's." I sat next to her on the bed and took her hand. I thought of Lorenzo, joyfully waiting at home. I thought of our own parents, of our friends. I thought of the years ahead of us. I thought about how a boundless joy could suddenly become a boundless sadness. I thought about Stella in her cradle with that little pink bow, and of how she was already different, though unaware of it, from all the other babies who were whimpering nearby.

I looked at Giulia and realized that she might be frightened for my sake. A mother can't flee from her child, but a father can, and indeed, it's been done so often. Men are frightened of other people's suffering. I know many a man who left his wife after she fell ill, or who made no effort to straighten out a wayward child. Suffering frightens men; it doesn't allow them to have total control. Yes, Giulia was right to be fearful for me.

When I walked out of the room, I stopped just outside the nursery. It was night by now, and given our special circumstances, they'd allowed the two of us to stay together a little longer than other couples. I stood facing the large window and peered through it at all the sleeping babies, finally spotting my little Stella. Now I could see what I hadn't seen before. And maybe even things that couldn't really be seen at all. Her eyes, the unusual shape they had, and that little potatolike nose. I placed one hand against the glass and slowly, slowly slid down

7

until I was sitting on the floor, my back against the wall of the nursery. The hallway was empty and only half lit. I could weep now, freely, with my back turned toward Stella. That way, she wouldn't see me, and I wouldn't see her.

It's been twelve years now since those first few days. And I fell in love with that fragile creature. And every dawn, watching the sun as it starts its journey, I think of her. I think of the moment when I'll wake her and of the big hug she'll give me. I think of the drive we'll take together, with her right next to me in the car. I don't hear, if I think about it, what we'll say to each other, but I do see her expressions. And they strike me as the extension of dawn.

Since my wife goes to work after we take off for the day, she can rise at her leisure. She's very focused on her career, and she seems distracted and distant. She can't stand Lorenzo's twenty-year-old lifestyle, and the only way she knows how to deal with Stella is to treat her like a helpless little animal. The two of us exchange very few words. We don't have much to say to each other. We can talk about what's going on in her job, how many houses she sold today, the praise people gave her, how real-estate stocks have shot up—but all this is utterly meaningless to me. About the lives that I encounter in the diaries I never utter even a peep. She doesn't seem interested in her own life, or in our life, let alone in those of others.

In the evenings it's mostly silent in our house. Giulia sits at the computer, Stella draws in her room, and Lorenzo tosses his basketball toward the basket that he put up above the door of his room. The boy has only a few passions: his sister, Italo Calvino, and Michael Jordan. The first he takes care of, the second he studies, and the third he idolizes.

In the park surrounding one of our city's more elegant residences there is a waterfall. In the summertime it's a lovely place to go, with its refreshing spray, and children delight in running up to it and then dashing off. This was Lorenzo's favorite place to go when Stella was born. It was there that I told him about her. He was just eight years old but he had always been a very wise, sensible child. His big eyes were forever seeking out things to understand, and his head was a storehouse of why's, and no reason given for anything ever satisfied him. He seemed to crave understanding.

And it was precisely my own quest for meaning and my respect for doubt, along with my deep fascination for research, that got me all wrapped up in the pages of one of my diaries. This diary's author was a mathematician who had been a disciple of Renato Cacciopoli, in Naples. He had lived intimately with numbers and with the wildly strange discovery of the great chain of infinities. Astronomers deal with infinities, seeking them and studying them. Philosophers imagine them, talk about them, invent them. But mathematicians make them come alive, can even walk up to them and touch them. The slim diary of this student of the great Neapolitan scholar aroused in me a passion for the topic. In it I ran across the marvelous life stories of so many mathematicians. In each story, the study of numbers, the obsession with seeking patterns, and the hierarchy of life's priorities were blended in an indescribably poetic fashion. I fell in love with the strange mathematical genius named Paul Erdös. I was enchanted by the religious quality of his relationship with numbers. I was charmed by the fact that he sought mathematical connections to everything, everywhere. He could turn up at any time of day or night at the homes of the greatest mathematicians in the world, sloppily dressed, wearing thick glasses, and with a few days' growth of beard, and he would announce, "My brain is open." I was struck by a tale told by the wife of a colleague of his who described how Erdös and her husband had sat stock still, deeply cogitating in front of a crowd at a meeting at the university, facing each other wordlessly for an hour and a half, at the end of which her husband had finally broken the silence, announcing triumphantly, "It's not zero; it's one." At which point everybody in the audience went crazy with joy.

There was another thing I recalled about the life of Erdös—it was the word he used for children. For him they were "epsilons," since in mathematics the Greek letter epsilon is the symbol that stands for tiny quantities.

Now I was alone with the epsilon of my own heart, just below a cool and gurgling waterfall. And I had to look into his big eyes and tell him a truth that would be difficult even for an adult to hear. I couldn't trick him; I wouldn't have been capable of doing so. We sat down next to the fountain as the sun was going down. Most people had already left the park, so we were nearly alone. On the other side of the waterfall a little girl in a purple T-shirt was having her father hold her up in such a way that she was able to stick her hands into the cascading water.

"Lorenzo, there's a problem," I said to him.

"I know," he replied. He said that although he was a child, I would have had to have a pretty low opinion of him if I thought he hadn't realized that fact. After all, neither his mother at the clinic nor I at home had been joyous in the way that people always are when a child is born. Or, more simply, we didn't exude the same happy air after the birth as we had when saying good-bye to him on our way to the hospital.

"What's wrong with Stella, Papà?"

That last word was the toughest one. It was simply too scary a word for me.

I myself had stopped using it when I was thirteen years old. One day, my father simply took off, closing the door behind him and disappearing. At home we couldn't even mention him. It was a tacit convention between my mother and me. I was afraid of her pain. I so clearly recall the nights I spent, without her seeing me, crouched down against the door of the bedroom in which Mamma was crying her heart out. And I too would bawl, but very very softly. And those tears were our unspoken agreement, the bond of silence between us, the river of the great removal that started already in the days right after his disappearance. His place at the table was removed, along with his napkin and his favorite glass. His clothes wound up, neatly packed, in the basement, alongside his papers. He left us just like that, one day, covering up all the traces of his path. From then on, only once in a while did we receive postcards showing sights we didn't know, postmarked from many cities in many far-off lands. Each time they would say the same thing: "I send you both my affection, Giacomo." His choice not to sign as "Papà" represented the obliteration of my existence. And so I seized on to that plural word "both," desperately clinging to the idea that it included me. But that other word, never once included in any of his postcards, has eaten away at me for my entire life.

And now here I am. I have to deliver a grim and brutal post-card, I have to write it in the optimal way, and the signature will never go away. "Stella is a different kind of child," I began.

Lorenzo flashed a surprised and somewhat harsh look at me. "Every child is different."

"Yes, but Stella has a problem that will cause her some delays—a problem that will make her understand things more slowly. Also, she'll have narrower eyes, like a Chinese girl. And she might speak poorly." I lowered my head, fearful of how he would reply.

"So you mean she's like Marco?"

"Yes, Lorenzo, she's like Marco."

There was a long and difficult silence. The only thing one could hear was the water of the falls, and far off, that little girl, now just a purplish dot, laughing and shouting, "Papà, put me down!" I turned around and saw Lorenzo was crying, but crying in a dignified fashion. I put my arm around his shoulder and pulled him up against me.

"Don't worry, Papà, I'll take care of her." And he told me that a swarm of ideas had suddenly passed through his head. Marco, his gentle but bad-smelling classmate. What his friends would say. He told me that all the kids felt ashamed of Marco's presence whenever they went on a school excursion. And that all the kids would one day feel ashamed of Stella, his sister. But then he added that he was ashamed of this thought. And that if Stella fell behind, then he, the closest of all to her, would wait for her.

I took him to the hospital. He hugged his Mamma tightly, and he said words of comfort to her. Then they brought Stella in. He looked at her in silence, confused. He gently touched the corners of her eyes with his fingers. He placed his index finger on her little potato nose and then he started to kiss her. In order to feign some kind of normalcy that wasn't there at all, I'd brought along a camera in order to capture forever the first moment of our family of four. I got everyone to look, framed the family portrait, set the flash, and snapped. When the photo was developed, I realized that I had captured the truth—that my wife was squeezing Stella too tightly, and, above all, that on his face Lorenzo had two big tears, plus a fake smile.

He never was jealous of Stella. I looked all over, including the Web, for first-person accounts written by parents of Down's-syndrome children. In many of them, siblings are quoted as repeatedly asking questions such as, "Why do you let *her* do things that you don't let *me* do?" or "Why are you always looking after *him* and never after *me*?", and so forth. But Lorenzo was Stella's big brother. And that day, beside the waterfall, he became a kind of father, a little father. When she was a toddler, he was the one who tucked her into bed. He was the one who told her bedtime stories, who played with her. And Stella is in love with this brother who lights up for her and for her alone.

In the meantime, Lorenzo has become quite taciturn. Very gradually he's been withdrawing. He's turned his room into a house. In it he has everything he needs—music and television, books and his hoop. He emerges only to go to the bathroom, to get himself a bite in the kitchen, and to go see Stella. And yet I can't blame him. There's such a silence in our house, such a frigidity of communication, that we rarely see one another at all. When we all eat together in the evening, only Stella holds forth, making noise, triggering our interest, our smiles, and our questions. In the background there's always the rumble of the TV, which often fills in for the silence on the part of those present. When Stella isn't at the table, having gone swimming or to speech therapy, there's only the drone of the words issuing from the screen.

And they are almost always gloomy words, crushers of hope. Is the world truly the way they portray it? One evening I was fascinated by a news item about the possible risk of tsunamis in lakes. The TV went on to report that the Chinese scientist Yao Tandung had discovered that the Himalayan glaciers are shrinking each year by the equivalent of the entire volume of the Yellow River. Further, the news report stated that in Switzerland, Austria, and Germany, certain ski resorts had covered up their glaciers with enormous sheets of white insulation, to try to save them. And just before the commercial, the newscaster added that between 1850 and today, the surface area of the world's ice caps has gone down by more than forty percent.

As I was watching my wife eating while she read a professional magazine, and my son lifting a forkful of spaghetti to his mouth, I thought about that diary whose author wrote of having scaled the majestic Grossglockner peak in Austria right after the end of World War II. He'd wanted to do it as an act of repentance, as if to exhibit, after all the darkness and horror of the war, the beauty of light and the grandeur of silence. After having seen hell, he wanted to see heaven from up close.

One time I took Stella up to the snow. She was a little darling, all bundled up. Lorenzo held her by the hand. She went crazy with delight over the sheets of white fluff. Thanks to her hood and sunglasses, she was even protected from the humiliating looks and the embarrassed smiles of strangers, and she savored a few hours of wild, unchecked joy. Giulia had stayed in the city for a work meeting but we three had just had the most beautiful day of our lives. That evening at dinner in the hotel, there was a rowdy group of vacationing friends at the table right next to ours. They were laughing and joking and making everyone else uncomfortable. At some point a toddler took advantage of a moment of silence, pointed his finger straight at Stella, and said to his mother, "Look, Mamma, a broken girl!"

There was an unreal silence. The mother started to rise and to come toward us. Lorenzo, who was around fifteen at the time, made a very firm gesture with his hand, and the woman stopped short without saying a word. I never knew whether Stella had understood, at least right then and there. That word, however, must have stayed lodged inside her, for she's repeated it many times in recent years. Whenever she would see a child with a limp or a patch over an eye, she'd ask if that child was broken like she was. That evening Lorenzo tucked her in, sat down beside her, and told her the story of a broken doll who was the most coveted of all by the children—because there wasn't any other one like her.

CHAPTER TWO

Today's dawn is gloomy; it's going to be a rainy day. On the television they announced that the amount of precipitation over these past few days has been very unusual for the season. In some areas of the country there have been huge floods, and in many European cities the rivers have overflowed their banks and spilled into the streets, sweeping away people and their belongings. I had a hard time waking up this morning, because yesterday Lorenzo waited until everyone was sleeping and then asked if I could talk with him for a little while. The mere fact that he wanted to do such a thing with me struck me as wonderful. We stayed together long into the night in this attic, looking out at a sky of swollen clouds illuminated by a strange light.

Everything was a result of his coming into the room, looking at me, casting a glance toward the TV, which, as always, was on, and saying, "No, I don't want to look at television!" Then, in a louder voice, he added, "I'm reading! I don't want to be disturbed!" And then he even shouted, "I'm starting to read the new novel by Italo Calvino!" And at last he smiled. He had expected that I would understand something that I didn't understand.

He explained to me that this last sentence was the opening sentence of a book by his favorite author. He was carried away by it in the way that youths are carried away by their latest love. He was delighted with the fact that Calvino's books were built on geometry and fantasy. Perfect constructions, mathematical combinations, painstakingly interlocked structures—but riddled with pure fantasy. The mathematics of dreams.

He was most excited to discover, while reading *If on a Winter's Night a Traveler*, the confirmation, in Calvino's words, of an image that had haunted him from the earliest days when he'd started to love and study the author's works. "Papà, when I was just beginning to devour those first novels, I always had in mind a certain object—a kaleidoscope. I'm telling you this because that was one of your first gifts to me—do you remember the long hours I spent playing with it? And now listen to what

Calvino writes: 'The moment I put my eye to a kaleidoscope, I feel that my mind, as the heterogeneous fragments of colors and lines assemble to compose regular figures, immediately discovers the procedure to be followed: even if it is only the peremptory and ephemeral revelation of a rigorous construction that comes to pieces at the slightest tap of a fingernail on the side of the tube, to be replaced by another, in which the same elements converge in a dissimilar pattern.'"

Lorenzo was dazzled by the structure of Calvino's novel *The Castle of Crossed Destinies*. It thrilled him that a grand story could be built on the themes of silence and symbols. That each of the travelers had arrived at the inn while under some kind of magical spell that had rendered them mute. That each one's ability to speak had been left behind in a vast forest, snagged on branches and brambles, flowers and thorns, during a voyage through a mysterious land. And that each one of them, upon realizing their state of muteness, used tarot cards to describe and reveal their inner thoughts. That is, it pleased Lorenzo that just one image could hold in it all the potential meanings of the greatest of human gifts: communication. Or rather, that in the arrangement of a number of tarot cards—mere images frozen on paper—there could be lurking a story or an entire life. Or then again, that a random jumble of presumably meaningful tarot cards thrown together on a table in an inn could in the end be rearranged to form a new pattern, a design imbued with its own perfect sense. And it pleased him that the traditional characters in Calvino's tale, his protagonists, never regained their normal voices but instead lived only through these symbols, and that their new voices were due entirely to a change of medium that restored the gift of meaning to them.

It was through Calvino that Lorenzo came across Raymond Queneau and was captivated by *Suburb and Fugue*. What he liked in that work was once again the idea that a dissatisfaction with one's own existence could give rise to a thousand possible lives. And the idea that pure fantasy could generate lives that were utterly unknown to the state registry of births and deaths.

He fell under the spell of these stories and he adored reciting them. In these nights—precious nights—of our exchanged ideas, I truly felt like a father. I had something that I'd never managed to have before, and I observed in this boy the traces, but more perfect, of my own dreads, dreams, and desires. There had once been a time in which I'd thought about changing the world, and who knows, perhaps, in some small way, I did. I don't have regrets, even if I'm somewhat disillusioned. But today my life is all here, in this attic and in the walls that define it. It is in these dawns that I await. It is in Stella, whose redemption and liberation from prejudices would be, for me, the greatest of all possible revolutions. It is in Lorenzo's dreams, in the stories that he pursues, in the passions that pervade his existence.

So that's my life, up to this point—its midpoint. And perhaps one day I, too, will write a diary and someone at the

National Archives will read it and my life will then be important, because it will no longer be solely my own.

Like Jacques L'Aumône, the hero of *Suburb and Fugue*, whom Lorenzo so reveres, I too am living several lives—the lives of those solitary authors who, by writing their diaries, entrusted to those vessels printed by some obscure press the most important message they knew: the ultimate meaning of the days, the hours, the joys, the pains, the passions, and the emotions that they experienced. They are my companions when I feel that everything is collapsing, or more precisely, when everything is pressing down on me. I have a dream that recurs, during the roughest nights. I see Stella rolling up the dawn as if it were a carpet, and hiding it, with her sweet smile, from my eyes. And there's my father's voice telling me to have faith, to wait for him; but it's a strangled, desperate voice—a cry for help, disguised as a promise of help.

I wake up drained, my eyes filled with tears. I have no one to call. I could do as Stella does when she's sad. I hear her through the nearly closed door and I can even see her through the crack. She kneels down on the floor, puts her hands together, and prays. She asks her "little God" to make Ginevra stop making fun of her, to bring some deskmate back to her desk at school, to make Lucia invite her to her birthday. And the "little God" sometimes helps her, sometimes doesn't. One evening I heard her say, "Little God, please try to make Mamma and Papà talk. They never say anything to each other." And when her prayer was over, I had the feeling that she turned toward the crack in the nearly closed door and smiled. That evening, perhaps I was the little God to whom she'd addressed her prayer.

I, likewise, prayed for my father to return. I missed him enormously. And most of all, I couldn't fathom why he had gone away. Where could he be, and with whom? Was he in danger? Had he found new loves? When I was a boy, I used to imagine him in the warm sun of a beach lined with palms or in a cabin surrounded by white snowbanks. Millions of times I wondered what he was doing right at the moment I was thinking about him. I imagined, or dreamed, that he'd delegated someone to monitor me, to follow me each day, to keep him informed about what I was like as I was growing up. Perhaps it was Uncle Giorgio, Mamma's brother, with whom he got along very well. But Uncle Giorgio was always taking trips to far-off places and he kept in touch only occasionally, and only by phone.

It was wonderful when we would all get together, in our country house. Not far outside the city our family had a cottage that my father, who is or was an architect, had remodeled. We would often go there, and over a Saturday and a Sunday, a kind of virtual time would get established, a party lasting forty-eight hours. There were always many friends, many colleagues of Papà. There were also their children, with whom I played on the meadow, and Uncle Giorgio, who organized lively games for us. My father had purchased this house in 1968, when he had become a tenured professor in the Faculty of Architecture.

But to celebrate his own career in those radicalized years struck him as wrong, and so he dubbed the place "House in the *sertão* [backwoods] that will one day be under water," borrowing this phrase from a film that had profoundly inspired him—a Brazilian film, made by a wacky but brilliant director by the name of Glauber Rocha. In the epic final scene of this film, according to Papà, the hero, a *cangaceiro* [bandit], dreams that the arid land might one day become a kind of paradise of evenly distributed wealth, a place of redemption for all oppressed people.

After Papà's disappearance, the house sadly did turn into a *sertão*. Visits took place less and less often. On the few occasions when our family assembled there with friends, a gaping hole would appear that our day-to-day life covered up. People would talk their way around certain subjects, trying not to bring up anything that might allude to the glaring absence. At least that's how it was when I was there with the grown-ups. Uncle Giorgio started turning up less often. He worked for a foreign airline and his trips were growing ever more frequent and of longer duration. Every so often he would give us a phone call, ask about our latest news, and try to cheer us up. But the house remained empty. It, too, was just like us, filled with happy memories between its walls but also a powerful sensation of emptiness everywhere.

Papà was, or is, a cheery soul. I recall him as being tall, with velvet slacks and a light blue shirt with rolled-up sleeves. And I recall his winter jackets, with oval-shaped leather patches on the elbows. I recall him reading many newspapers, and I recall that in the wake of the political upheavals of 1968, he'd slowly given up on that era's grand dreams and high ideals and replaced them with an almost ostentatious detachment, a clearly proclaimed disillusionment. He walked away on a day in March in the mid-1970s. And still now, nearly thirty years later, I don't know why. And this is what I find unbearable. A father can die, a father can go off with another woman, a father can move to another continent, but a father cannot simply disappear, cannot erase himself and others along with him, cannot turn himself into nothing but memories and absence.

In the catalogue of all possible destinies, one of the most difficult and strange ones had befallen me: to search, and never to stop searching, for my entire life.

One Sunday morning Lorenzo woke up at dawn, as I had. He came into the attic holding a small book—a book by Calvino, needless to say. It was a set of essays about fables. In one of them, in particular, about the "map of metaphors," Calvino describes how Basile, the author of the *Pentameron*, was obsessed by the idea of dawn, how for him it was a kind of required punctuation, which, obeying a "syntactic and rhythmic necessity, serves to indicate a pause and a reprise, an ending and a return to the beginning."

In the same essay Calvino recalls how Benedetto Croce, in his introduction to Basile's rich catalogue, had extracted four "selected dawns" from it. Calvino extends Croce's list with his own nearly endless series of phrases such as "Whenever Night banishes all birds, promising a handsome reward to whosoever brings her news of a flock of remote black shadows," or then again, "As soon as the Sun came to visit, all shadows that had been placed in prison by the court of Night were released...." Lorenzo, showing me these sentences, smiled. They were a confirmation of his opinion. Namely, that Calvino was not a writer, but that his universe, disseminated far and wide, was a way to apprehend and experience life—a new kind of catechism. That his works, if read with the proper spirit, were a manual of recipes for being alive. This assumes, of course, that life is not to be lived just for oneself, which is easy, but in order to merge oneself with a thousand other lives. Always to be many selves and never to be alone, even when one is.

Calvino is thus for Lorenzo almost a religion based on reason, a spiritual guide. Poking fun at himself, Lorenzo therefore claims to be a "Calvinist," and he asserts that it's no coincidence that he was born in the same year as the author died—clearly a passing of the baton. And he also claims that if he didn't have the author's company, if he didn't experience the thrill of doors being opened wide every time by Calvino's words, if he hadn't gotten lost a thousand times in Calvino's mazes and found himself a thousand times in Calvino's dreams, then life would seem even more useless to him.

He asked me: "Which dawn in Basile's catalogue is most like today's, Papa?" I looked up at the sky, heavy with its somber dawn, and ran down the table of contents of Lorenzo's little book. "This one," I said. And I showed him: "Dawn had gone out to oil the wheels of the Sun's chariot and, from the exertion of using a stick to remove the grass from the wheel's hub, had grown as red as a scarlet apple." I liked the idea of Dawn exerting herself, a kind of contradiction in terms.

That morning we spent quite a while talking about Stella, as usual. Lorenzo told me what had happened the previous evening. They'd been alone at home. Their mother had had to show an apartment to some clients, and I had gone to a public presentation of the diary of a man who'd flown halfway around the world in a glider.

Lorenzo had heard a cry coming from Stella's room. Then she started to call out in a voice strangled by fear. He rushed to his sister. When he opened the door he found her kneeling on the floor, her hands covered with blood dripping all over her legs. She looked at him in terror, embarrassment, and confusion. He put his arms around her, and while he was hugging her he told her about it, he told her that everything was all right, that this happened to all girls of her age. But she asked him why this blood was coming out of her, and why from right there. Was she dying? He smiled at her and said she wasn't, that this blood was proof that she was growing up, that now she was a real girl and not just a little kid. "Does blood make you grow?" asked Stella. Lorenzo didn't know what to say to her, partly because he suddenly realized for the first time that Stella might never become a mother, might never give rise to another life—that instead she might simply live her whole life alone. And soon he was cleaning her up, with his hand's timid gestures betraying his great embarrassment. He found some sanitary pads in their mother's bathroom and placed one of them on Stella's underwear. When she saw it she said to him, "You see, you're not telling me the truth, are you? I'm not growing, I'm going backwards. You're putting me back in diapers, but I grew out of them a long time ago."

Lorenzo smiled at her. They lay down together on her bed and, still hugging, put on a film to watch. It was *What's Up, Doc?*, their favorite—a story of swapped suitcases, mistaken identities, and chase scenes taking place in the streets of San Francisco, with its steep hills and its cable cars filled with people dangling from their sides.

"Lorenzo, when I'm big, will you take me there? Do you promise you will?" Lorenzo replied that he would definitely take her—and that since from tonight on she was big, she should be ready to go soon.

At this point in Lorenzo's narrative, his mood shifted from tense to joyous. He told me that I'd been unlucky from the moment of my birth. That it was bad enough to have had my father disappear, my wife grow distant from me, a daughter with Down's, and a very solitary son, but that the course of my life was all predestined by my date of birth. He said the day of the year was good, in fact perfect, but the year itself was not. I'd come late, as always. As always, I'd lost my chance for the best

27

possibility. And he told me that on March 2, 1962, the very same date and month as my birth, but two years earlier, the world had undergone a significant acceleration, before a crowd of 4,124 spectators assembled in the sports arena in the small town of Hershey, Pennsylvania, famous for being a chocolate capital. That evening of sweet magic, in front of an ecstatic crowd, Wilt Chamberlain, the center for the Philadelphia Warriors, sank 100 of the 169 points that gave his team a victory over the New York Knicks. He shot and scored, flew and scored again. And bit by bit the crowd started to realize that they were witnessing a legendary performance, which, more than forty years later, would become part of the life of a boy on a remote continent. When the last period was about to end, each time the Warriors gained possession, the crowd would scream, "Give it to Wilt!" Everyone in the crowd would participate, and Wilt didn't disappoint. When he sank his hundredth point, neither more nor less, the whole place went wild. And in his room Lorenzo has a poster, purchased on one of his yearly summer vacations in the United States, in which Wilt, one of the few blacks in basketball at that time when the sport was still nearly all white, is holding a small piece of paper with a handwritten "100" on it. He looks very pleased, but also reserved and dignified.

For Lorenzo, basketball has become a reason for living. He adores the fact that time is counted backward toward zero, that each of the hundreds of shots during a game could turn out, at the end of the game, to have been crucial, that everything could still, even just one second before the forty-minute period ends, be riding in the balance—as in life. One gesture, one idea, one mistake, one careless act can raise or smash hopes. He loves the way that basketball is a mixture of imagination and team-work, that a player can fly and float in the air before dunking the ball in the hoop. He likes the key role played by numbers, percentages, statistics. He takes pleasure in this pastiche of poetry and precision, of inspiration and bookkeeping, of diagrams drawn on a board and utter, spontaneous genius. He delights in the unpredictability of a play that comes together in the very last moments of a game. Basically, it's something that resembles the structure of so many Calvino novels, says Lorenzo.

It was Sunday, that special Sunday. The television was announcing, as dawn was disappearing, the spread of bird flu and the state of alarm all across Asia to Russia, and it alluded to the Spanish flu, which had killed so many millions of people shortly after World War I. The editorial of the most widely read news-paper, which was usually focused on politics or the economy, was deeply concerned with the matter of sneezing chickens. After all, they could evolve into agents capable of unleashing something so catastrophic that "we will regret every single sum-mer day not spent in the search for a cure, and in comparison, the Iraq mess, the high price of oil, and the greenhouse effect will all seem like good news."

To Lorenzo it seemed, fundamentally, that this was the paradox of our era. That despite all of our deep science, our computers, and our genetic engineering, we are still powerless in the face of upheavals by nature. That tsunamis, hurricanes, global warming, and the spread of medieval-style fevers and epidemics all reflect an unchanging world.

"You know, Papà, I saw a photo of all of you on the day of the housewarming party for the country place. The grown-ups look as if they come from another epoch, if you compare them with the photos of the party when I was born, less than twenty years ago. Different clothes, different eyeglasses, different haircuts. As if society had moved very quickly, the way it did between World War II and 1968. You were all running; everyone ran. And the wind was visible in your hair, in your clothes. But if I look at you now and compare you to a photo from the mid-eighties, I get the impression that you adults are all unchanged. Sure, you have more technological gadgets now, but your language, especially the language of your clothes and your attitudes, even your body language, reveals a slowing-down. Things haven't changed much. On the other hand, almost thirty years since those days, what's become of the moon, of space exploration, of humanity conquering new frontiers? We're in a simulation, a virtual reality, Papà—just like the rides in Disneyland. We're sure that we're going at supersonic speeds, but in fact we're standing stock still. And bird flu and other viruses are knocking at the doors of our houses. And they scare us to death."

"Fear is what dominates our lives, Lorenzo. Fear of terrorist attacks, of diseases, of nature. Fears abound—including minor ones. People fear that having stored their whole life in the memory of a computer, some virus—in this case, a computer virus—could just gobble it all up, leaving them empty and naked, without a trace remaining. It's a feeling of oppression, of control. Someone unknown to us can observe all the purchases we've made, can find out the diseases we suffer from, can read our email, can even track our whereabouts, thanks to cell phones. We've all got rooms in the inn of fear. Of course my father would have had a tougher time vanishing without a trace today, but that's hardly a big consolation."

Lorenzo had been deeply struck by a story that took place in England, and which, for a while, had been occupying the front pages of all the papers. One spring morning, a young man of about twenty had been found, soaked and frightened, on the beach of the Isle of Sheppey, in Kent. He was unable to say his name or tell what had happened to him. After being taken to a hospital, he was still confused, dazed, and unable to speak. The labels had been ripped off his clothes and his shoes didn't give any indication of their place of origin. When a psychologist handed him a sheet of paper and a pen, he flawlessly drew a grand piano with a stool, even with all the shadows properly rendered. So then he was escorted to a piano, and he started to play classical music in a charming fashion, or indeed, "marvelously well," as another psychologist phrased it. Nonetheless, playing music didn't break his silence.

"So," said Lorenzo intensely, "I see three possibilities.

Number one: he's a great impostor who figured out the best possible way to gain fame for himself. If this were the case, he would disgust me, but so would our society, which drives people to such pathetic lengths to gain publicity. But for the time being, what really disgusts me is myself, because my immediate reaction, through habit, was to jump to the conclusion that the truth isn't what you see in front of you, but a hidden, ugly, sneaky, cynical alternative.

"Case number two: the guy is sick. Perhaps he's autistic. But somehow there's no one, even in this day of the shrinking globe, who recognizes him. It's not possible that this guy doesn't have a mother or father, a brother, an aunt, some kind of relative—a schoolmate, a playmate, a friend, an old girlfriend, a neighborhood, a school, an orchestra. Not possible that he never had a history teacher or a music teacher. Not unless he's an alien. So somehow, for some reason, there's a conspiracy of silence around the fellow. Perhaps we're all responsible for the trauma that took away his voice. And in that case, it's a horror story.

"Then there's a third possibility, Papà—that the guy did know all those kinds of people and they're all looking for him now, but they live in a land where there's some kind of blind spot in the great global communications network. It's a weird place with no television reception, a place where no newspapers ever come, a place deprived of computers and the Web. The silence around him might be telling us that somewhere in the world there's a 'non-place' where people talk only among themselves, exchanging experiences in their lives, but where they don't know the great 'express train' of the world, which loudly gobbles up everything that it runs into.

"So far so good. But then, there came a point where the truth emerged—a truth that blew all my guesses to hell. One morning a nurse walked into his room and said to him, as she said every morning, 'So, are you going to talk today?' And he looked up at her and answered, 'Yes, I think I am.' And he opened up, at long last. It turned out he was German and that he had worked in Paris, where his gayness caused fewer problems. But he'd lost his job and decided to make a break, taking a train for London. Once off the train he got lost and drifted about dazedly with blurry visions of suicide in his head. And in that state, so he claimed, he'd been found. Then, on a whim, he decided not to talk anymore. The fellow, as it later turned out, came from a well-to-do family of builders in Germany. And he chose to draw the piano simply because it was 'the first thing that sprang to my mind.' And there's no truth to the claim that he'd played 'marvelously.' He'd just banged on two keys, in a very boring way, for a long time.

"So reality crafted a fourth variation—the most cynical one of all, in which everyone is as bad as they can possibly be. The guy himself, who invented this idea of staying mum, and who calculated when to lose his voice and when to find it again. His rich family, who couldn't possibly have failed to see his picture in one or another of the numerous decent newspapers, but who all kept silent, probably in order to save 'the company's good name' from being tarnished by a scandal about their estranged gay son. And lastly, all those fine headshrinkers in Kent, who concocted the tale of the 'wondrous' pianist. It's all repulsive, but it's typical of our times."

I replied, trying to make him feel better, that this story of "Piano Man," as the fellow had been dubbed by the papers, is a Calvino-style story. And Lorenzo replied that the same thing had occurred to him. That at the beginning of *The Castle of Crossed Destinies*, the voyagers realize that no sounds are escaping their lips because "the passage through the forest had cost each of us our faculty of speech." And that when they were hit by "the agony of not being able to exchange the many experiences that each of us yearned to communicate," that's when a pack of playing cards—the tarot cards—appeared on the table. And those cards thus became, in that mute but not-deaf world, the key to communication, to speaking, to having a past.

Just then, as dawn was coming to an end, we heard a sound. It came from Stella's room. We were worried, recalling the traumatic event she'd gone through the night before. It seemed too early for her Sunday to be beginning. And yet the attic door opened and there she stood, right in front of Lorenzo and me. She was all dressed up in her finest clothes and in her hand she was holding a small traveling bag.

"Lorenzo, I'm ready. Are we going to go where all those chases were? You promised me."

Lorenzo smiled. And he assured her once more that he would take her there, and soon. But first Stella would have to finish school and he would have to pass many exams. This made her sad, but as a consolation she was told that all three of us would look at the film once more, together. And as each new scene started, she would ask, "And will you take me to *this* place, too?"

CHAPTER THREE

Summer came and Lorenzo kept his word. He was a sensible boy, he'd made many trips to the United States, and he didn't want to break the promise he'd made his sister. There was no reason they shouldn't go. Stella was happier than I'd ever seen her at the idea of doing this grown-up thing, and Lorenzo no less so. Both of them, as they closed the front door behind them, would be taking a very major step forward. But Giulia was against it, and this contributed to lowering her popularity with the children. It was I who made the decision. I drove them to the airport and watched them check in. When they turned around, I wished I had a camera in my eyes to capture Stella's smile, her eyes already leaving behind everything she'd known before, and her chubby little hand waving in a nearly mechanical fashion.

And Lorenzo, with his sweet and melancholy smile, brandished in the air the book that he'd brought along for the trip to America—*Six Memos for the Next Millennium* by Italo Calvino.

That lonely summer, the days were long and difficult. The dawns didn't satisfy me, and in addition to the colors spraying out of the television, there was the light of the computer screen on which news of my two offspring reached me. Giulia had gone off to a beauty farm and I understood, or rather, I strove to understand, that in this woman, my woman, something had broken when Stella was born. She, being a little older than I, had insisted that we have another child. But the child had come "broken" and Giulia took on the burden of guilt for that imperfect small life. Her exaggerated concerns during the first few years were followed by a careful withdrawal from the situation, though it was never total. But she was turning cold and hard and was looking elsewhere, trying to find some meaning to her life, which was slipping by all too quickly. I understood her, but we didn't have much to say to each other anymore. In fact, we no longer said anything at all to each other.

The television reported that we were experiencing the hottest summer in history. That in Alaska, in these days of August, the temperature was in the mid-eighties and that the permafrost, the indispensable foundation for the equilibrium of that part of the biosphere, was rapidly vanishing. Meanwhile, far around the world, the Gobi Desert was growing—statistics were displayed in a superposition of graphs—at the rate of four thousand square miles per year.

I thought of the long vacations we'd spent at our summer place, the *casa del sertão*, when Papà was still among us. And all at once a sense of guilt welled up in me for having abandoned the place. It was just that the absences between those walls had been unbearable. And in my childhood memories, that place had been so tightly associated with periods of total serenity, just as in later years it became identified with gloom, loneliness, and emptiness. No one had been back there for many years. I hadn't had the heart to sell it, especially after the death of my mother. To tell the truth, its state of abandon struck me as a very apt reflection of the meanings that the house had taken on in our lives. It was the house of "the sea that had become a back-woods"—just the opposite of what it should have been and could have been, and of what it had been for us, for all of us.

One day, out of the blue, the house seemed to be pulling me. Perhaps it was my physical aloneness those days, or perhaps it was that day's plain, boring dawn without any spark or hint of meaning. Perhaps it was the fact that every time either of my children said the word "Papà" it hit me in my gut like a fist smashing against a plasterboard wall. Or perhaps it was that all of a sudden that house, a symbol of bleakness in my mind, took on the feeling of a jewelbox filled with possible reasons, hints, and meanings, which just might shed light, for the first time, on how and why my life had been torn asunder.

And so, as dawn drew to an end, I walked out of the apartment and headed off by car into the deserted city. I drove all the way across it, left the city limits, and after a while found myself at the villa's gate. Despite some trouble I had managed to locate the keys, and I looked for one that might open a lock that had been closed for perhaps decades. The gate swung open and I set eyes on the garden, the very garden in which I used to play ball with Uncle Giorgio, now just a wild tangle of greenness—trees, hedges, and brambles—all twisted together. If possible, the place was even more beautiful than it had been before—more mysterious, more intricate, more complex. The ivy had overrun nearly the entire façade of the house, and the trees' branches were leaning down onto the wooden trellis, under which, in nice weather, we used to eat. Dazzling flashes of memory brought back to mind images of those happy days, in just the places where I was now walking.

"Angkor"—somehow this name sprang to my mind. And I recalled the diary of an Italian archaeologist who had worked in that enchanted spot in the Cambodian jungle. A city that had been the center of a powerful empire, built upon an ingenious system of artificial canals that furnished water for rice paddies and fields of vegetables. A city built according to a cosmic logic, surrounded by walls that defined the very edges of the universe. Angkor Wat was a majestic palace, covering nearly a square mile, with spires that rose as high as two hundred yards, and endlessly decorated walls. The palace died, along with the civilization that had fashioned it, in the middle of the fifteenth century. And from that time on, the jungle had grown over it and for hundreds of years it had remained unseen by human eyes. And thus it stayed, in silence, beneath the rain and the fog. The jungle kept on growing, covering, and hiding, until a young Frenchman, Henri Mouhot, came across the spot in 1860. The Italian archaeologist, in his own diary, quotes Mouhot's diary entries recording his fantastic nineteenth-century voyage. "At last, after three hours of walking on a path covered by a deep bed of powder and fine sand, cutting through a dense jungle . . . exhausted from the heat and a very rough passage through quicksand, we stopped to rest in the shade of great trees, and it was then that, as I cast my glance eastwards, I was astounded by the unexpectedness and charm of what I saw." It was Angkor, which was about to flourish again after four hundred years, having survived time, having been made eternal through its solitude. The city with its palace emerged within and out of the jungle. The astonished discoverer related: "One cannot imagine anything more beautiful than this architecture, lurking deep in the jungle, in one of the most remote regions of the world, uncivilized, unknown, deserted, where the tracks of wild animals have replaced those of humans, where all that one hears is the roaring

of tigers, the rasping of elephants, and the bellowing of stags."
I would have loved to have been that man, to have experienced
that marvel. But now here I am in my own little Angkor.

Somewhere there was a tree on which Uncle Giorgio used
to record my height. He would make me stand there, one hand
on my head. And then came the best moment—I would slip out
from under his gentle touch and look on as he measured the
height and carved the numerals into the bark of the tree with
his pocket knife. That tree had to be around here somewhere.
I moseyed about at a slow pace, so as not to miss out on any
of the physical sensation that I was experiencing of revisiting
the past. I would take a step, then stop. And the whole time I
was being hit by intense memory flashes and feeling like a child
and an old man, both at once. And then suddenly, there it was,
just to the left of the house, looking as if its branches—an infinity of them—were weighing it down. And like everything else,
it was much smaller than I remembered. I found the carved
numerals, still readable. They started in March of 1968, when I
was four, and they ended with the triumphant announcement
"one meter fifty," in February of 1977. One month before the
day. And the tree, when you came down to it, was telling
the truth. My real growth had in fact stopped at that point, and
that mark on the tree recorded our final visit, with all of us
together, to the *casa del sertão*.

Later, when we went back there, the absence had swallowed
up any desire to stop the passage of time. It wouldn't have

occurred to anyone to pretend that things were still the way they had been. I placed my hand on the tree and ran my finger along the numerals carved into its trunk. From there, leaning my back against the bark, I could survey the whole house. It was really in terrible shape. Silent, stately, and decaying—and yet imbued with some kind of magic. The ivy that had grown all over it lent it a dreamlike quality, and the play of reflected light unexpectedly endowed it with a sparkling appearance. After gliding my fingers nostalgically over the nameplate, I walked in, brushing aside the branches and leaves that dangled down in front of the door. And then a memory flash brought back to me, for the first time, the image of the picture that we'd snapped on the day of the housewarming—a color photo brimming with life, showing people moving about, joking and celebrating, making sure that no one was left out. It was Uncle Giorgio who'd snapped it. And in that flashback I once again saw people with long hair, and eyeglasses with dark, heavy frames. I saw lit cigarettes and overcoats from a time long gone, parkas, and duffle coats. I saw girls with strange hairdos, blends of the sixties style and the radical-student style. And I saw that nameplate, brought triumphantly by my father, which looked to me as if it was glowing at all four of its corners, like an advertisement.

I started to explore inside the house, which was lit by that special kind of light that penetrates dark nooks with luminous cones and brings along with it, or rather reveals, dust in motion—millions of tiny specks, frantically flipping and spinning. Perhaps their frenzy comes solely from the joy of being lit up, rediscovered, observed. I took a turn around the empty rooms. On the floor there were some newspapers dating from the early eighties, a few architecture magazines, and boxes all ready for packing up the emptiness. I walked into my old room, not easily recognizing it. At my feet there were a few children's books. And there was *Moby Dick*, which I'd read in that room, savoring it week after week, returning eagerly each time to pick up the tale again. All at once it hit me that in this special haven with its suspended sense of time, and perhaps only here, it might make sense for me to share in Ishmael's quest, in his hunt for the whale and its multiple meanings, in his hunt for its marvelous and awesome essence, both vulnerable and unassailable.

Up on one wall, having for some unclear reason survived all this time, was the poster that Papà had wanted to stick up for the first anniversary of our house. It showed two black American athletes at the Olympics, each with his head bowed and his right fist in a black glove, clenched and raised in the air. The poster was still there, an anachronistic symbol of resistance against the passage of time, slightly curled up at the corners, with the faces so worn away that they were no longer recognizable.

My parents' bedroom was next to mine. I walked in and had to cover my eyes to shield them from the brilliant light spilling in through the openings that once had been splendid windows through which one enjoyed a beautiful view of the garden, the trees, and the greenery. The room was now empty. But in one corner, incredibly, there was a telephone, and strewn nearby were a few telephone books from 1980. Made of black bakelite, this was one of those heavy, old, severe-looking phones, the kind whose receiver sat on a base that looked like a boat with little poles sticking up at all four corners. And this boatlike base would float upwards or sink down, depending on whether the phone was in use or not. It was an ancient telephone that we'd brought from home. And I still remember why Papà, before he received his tenured professorship, had inserted a little lock into one of the holes on the dial—it was to prevent people from making too many calls. It occurred to me that the durability of this phone was, once again, a symbol of the changing times. Back in those years, people had shorter lives and objects had longer ones. Today we're consumed by a frenzied desire to replace old things with new ones, to toss even youthful objects into the garbage can, catching them by surprise.

That telephone had made it through three decades and now all it did was absorb, with its shiny black coat, all the sunbeams that came bashing into it.

I crouched down and lifted the receiver. In the earpiece I heard a dial tone indicating that the line was available. No one had come out here for many, many years. I had never paid a thing for this line. I had no memory of having cut the service; it had to have been my mother who had taken care of that. But that sound reaching my ear, in that empty room in a deserted house, was a bolt from the blue. I dialed several numbers. First my office, then home, but nothing went through. I flipped through the phone books, teasing my memory, searching for names of friends from those days, and trying out their numbers. But the telephone, quite properly, reacted mutely to all these attempts. They were all six-digit numbers, and even when I pre-fixed them with the useless city code, all I got was an obvious, natural, reasonable silence. I replaced the receiver, put down the phone books, and got up to leave. But then I hesitated for a moment, and went back. I wanted to extend the game, to make just one last try, and so I dialed the number of the old house where we'd lived in the city. I simply felt tempted by the idea of carrying out the same ritual as way back then, when I went to visit friends or my grandparents. I liked the idea of dialing that magical number that I had so loved back then, for two reasons. For one thing, it had seven digits, and also the digits had a melodic lilt, first rising and then suddenly cutting off. And so I dialed, very slowly, "eight-four-five-six-zero-nine-two"—no two digits the same, and with that zero near the middle. Paul Erdös would have had a field day exploring the meaning of that sequence. The final digit was very short, almost a chop. When the circular dial rotated back to its rest position and my finger slipped out of the little hole for the number "two," I was dumb-struck to hear, all at once, a familiar sound—the sound of a ring, the sound that makes you imagine that in some far-off house, thanks to a motion you made with your hand, a telephone is ringing and someone has interrupted whatever they were doing and is now walking over to answer. The telephone was ringing; who ever could have taken over our old number?

How come it worked without the city code? How come all the other numbers I'd dialed had resulted in total silence? I started to feel strange; I didn't understand. The telephone was ringing and each pause between one ring and the next felt like an eternity, just as it felt like a winter or a whole lifetime between the moment when the ringing was suddenly cut short and the next moment, in which I heard—in which I outrageously heard—a voice, a boy's voice. "Hello?" he said, with a slightly shrill timbre that made him sound about twelve or thirteen years old. But my own voice failed me; my throat squeezed shut. "Pronto, hello, who's there?" he repeated. And I put down the receiver.

I couldn't speak. My heart was throbbing and an unbearable confusion had invaded my being. I took a deep breath, saying to myself that none of this made any sense at all, wondering how that long-dead telephone could have sprung back to life solely for that ancient, seven-digit number, without any city code. I tried to put things together in my mind. I wondered if it might somehow be a toll-free number, but even if it were, I couldn't figure out why the phone would work only with that number and no others. Just to make sure, I tried a few others, ones I knew by heart, such as the number for emergencies or the number to call in order to put a hold on a stolen credit card.

And then I remembered my cell phone. I picked it up and redialed the number where the boy had answered. Nothing. Not a sound, not a peep. Then I shakily went back to the black bakelite telephone. I once again picked up the receiver and redialed the number that should have been invalid—invalid like my family, invalid like the house in which I lived, invalid like this very telephone of yore, against which, insanely, I was pressing my left ear, an ear that had grown accustomed to hearing sounds of the new millennium.

Despite my flustered state, I had somehow figured out a plan—a plan of attack. The phone at the other end was ringing again. But this time, it took fewer rings until the boy's voice answered once again. And this time, he sounded a little more peeved. "Pronto?" he said, heavily stressing the initial "pr." I took a deep breath and said very quickly, "Pronto, who's this?" The boy, caught off guard, replied, "Astengo household." But I quickly hung up once again, feeling ashamed of myself.

Who was this boy who shared my last name? Where was he? How could he have the telephone number that I used to have thirty years ago? And why on earth was that the only number that this disconnected bakelite phone could reach? I didn't know what to do or what to think. I stopped for a moment of reflection, to digest these strange new facts. I paced back and forth in this bedroom brightly lit by intense sunlight, with those myriad specks of dust whirling crazily all about me. I tried to make time pass. I ran through various possible things to say the next time I called, including the most ridiculous, irrational schemes.

After half an hour had gone by, or maybe a little longer, I dialed the number again. The boy answered as before, but this time he was calmer. Thinking I was verging on craziness, I said, "Pronto, is this the Astengo household?" "Yes," he replied, matter-of-factly. In that half hour, I'd gone over every possibility, planned out every imaginable line to fit every imaginable scenario, and now, although I was nervous, I stayed cool. I decided to go for the most extreme, the most ridiculous of all my guesses, despite being sure that it would turn out wrong and that everything had a rational, reasonable, natural explanation, though I might never know what it was.

I said, "Is this Giovanni?" and as I uttered these words I realized I was heading into the twilight zone. Here I was, using a dead telephone line, in a house deserted for decades, asking a boy who was replying to my old home number from thirty years ago whether he was myself. But he quickly reassured me, "Yes, it's me."

So I was speaking with myself. For some reason this old telephone line had made a connection not across space but across time. And that old house had somehow, miraculously, remained connected with the days in which it had been lived in, inhabited. Days in which that ritual gesture, the dialing of that number, was frequent and natural. I had no idea what was happening to me, and I was sweating, but I didn't let myself get caught by surprise when he asked me, "And who am I speaking to?" I was prepared for the question, and had a response ready. Since this was the craziest of all the scenarios I'd turned over in my mind, I'd placed it on my brain's most remote and most hidden shelf. But now I made a mad dash to retrieve it.

"This is Uncle Giorgio, Giovanni."

"Uncle!" joyously exclaimed the boy—or rather, myself. "Was that you, earlier?"

"Yes, it was, but we got cut off. You know, I'm quite far away."

"Where are you, Uncle?"

I cleared my voice in order to gain a bit of time, and then answered, "In New York, Giovanni."

"How are you doing?" he asked me warmly.

But I didn't have time for chitchat. I had to find out instantly the year, month, and day in which Giovanni—or rather, myself—was living. I had to find out whether Papà was still at home or had left us, and I had to find out whether Giovanni—or rather, myself—was alone at home or not.

"I'm fine, Giovanni, fine. I'm working very hard. Say, do you know that today I saw the American president drive by in a long parade of cars?"

"You mean Carter?" he replied, in that well-informed manner so typical of the youngster I myself had once been.

"Yes, exactly." And so we were somewhere in the four-year period between January of 1977 and the end of 1980. Papà had left us on March 13, 1977. Any explicit question on that topic

that I asked would reveal me as the impostor that I was. I certainly couldn't be unaware about whether Papà was still around or not, nor about any other important family matter.

While I was ad-libbing other bits of random chitchat about my latest flight and my fellow passengers, about airports and passports, I was trying to find a way to wangle some key facts out of him. And then it came to me. "Say, Giovanni, do you have a newspaper there at home? Somehow the papers didn't get delivered here today."

He replied, "I think so, but it would be yesterday's. Papà always brings it when he comes home in the evenings."

"Well, could you go get it and read me the headlines? I want to know what's going on in Italy."

"Sure—just a minute."

He didn't call out to anyone—a sign that he was home alone. Moreover, he'd said that Papà brings home the paper every evening, which implied two things: that my father hasn't yet gone away, and that the time of day is afternoon, when Mamma and Papà are always at work and when I used to stay at home, in charge of everything. But what I was still lacking was the precise date. Nonetheless, I'd taken a major step forward: we were somewhere in the period preceding March 13, 1977.

He returned to the phone and said, "I found it. What would you like me to read to you?"

"The headlines," I replied, hoping they would supply me with very specific information.

Giovanni started out. "Okay, fine. The main headline says, 'Moro launches a challenge: Just try to put the Christian Democrats on trial.' Then in the middle of the front page it says, 'Northern Italy paralyzed by a strike of fuel-truck drivers.' And then at the bottom—but of course you know this—it says, 'Panic in Washington: City Hall occupied by terrorists. Islamic sect attacks the headquarters of the Jewish Defense League, the Islamic Center, and City Hall.'"

Well, the Moro headline could only refer to the Lockheed flap. This had been in 1977, but I didn't recall which month. Then I had a sudden flash of inspiration and asked Giovanni, "Are you sure it's yesterday's paper? Check the date."

"Wait a second—yes, it's yesterday's. Thursday, March 10, 1977."

My God. Something, somebody was bringing me into contact with myself as a kid, at that crucial turning point when my entire existence turned upside down. Something, somebody was allowing me to talk with myself as a boy, at only forty-eight hours' remove from the disappearance of my father. It was absurd, but it was happening. That voice was mine, that candor was my own.

"How did school go today?" I asked, trying to gain time.

"They handed back my Italian assignment. I got the first '10' I've ever had in middle school!"

"Was that for your prose paraphrase of Leopardi's *Ricordanze?*"

"Yes," he replied, and then, after a pause, "But how would you know that?"

I felt a burst of panic and said, "You told me so, didn't you?"

"No, Uncle, it's been a week since we last spoke."

"Well then, probably it was Mamma or Papà—I don't recall. Are you pleased with your work?" He didn't have to reply, because I vividly remembered the incredible joy I'd felt on receiving that grade. I recall that for it, my father gave me a soccer shirt that turned out to be too small, which greatly pained me. And I also perfectly recall how I told him the grade on his arrival at home. But I wanted to be reminded of it by my own self, so I asked Giovanni, "Have you told Papà about your '10' yet?"

"No," he replied. "Listen to this, Uncle—I decided to give him a surprise. I've made a set of little cards with the numbers from one to ten. On each card there's an arrow pointing to the next card, and the last arrow points into my room. There I'll be waiting for him with my textbook open to the page where it has Leopardi's words, 'Faint stars of Ursa Major, never did I think I would return to gaze upon you....' And then comes my favorite part of all: 'And what immense thoughts, what sweet dreams came to me, inspired by the sight of that far-off sea, those blue mountains, that I spy from here, and that one day I imagined crossing—mysterious worlds, carrying mysterious joys to my soul....' He won't know what it's all about, and so then I'll reveal it all. What do you think, Uncle Giorgio?"

"I think it's a terrific idea. I'm sure he'll give you a present for it."

"Let's hope so," replied Giovanni.

"But tell him to make sure he gets the right size."

"How come?" he asked me, mystified.

"Oh, I don't know, you know how absentminded your father is . . . By the way, how is Papà doing these days?" I asked him, trying to determine whether my father was troubled or in distress, or had withdrawn into himself.

"He's doing well—in fact, great. He went through a pretty rough period, but now he's happy and is always joking. Why do you ask?"

"Oh, just wondering, Giovanni. So tell me what *you're* up to."

And so Giovanni described a day taken straight out of my thirteenth year. He told me he'd come home from school, eaten lunch while reading a "Diabolik" comic book, and watched a bit of television. Then he'd started to play a special game of his own involving poker chips, which he'd reconceived as soccer players. He took all the round chips of a given color, wrote numbers on them in pencil, laid them out in precise tactical formation on the table, and used two larger, rectangular chips for the goalposts. Then he looked around for a smaller chip that could serve as the ball, and then came the kickoff. It's an amazing memory that I still cherish from those long-gone days—the feeling of a new world, a fantasy world, where a mere poker chip could become Zoff or

Pulici, Pruzzo or Antognoni. And where your physical movements—but also your honesty—would determine the outcome
of the challenge. In fact, if you moved your opponent's goalie
just a bit too late when your own team was shooting for a goal,
you'd seal his fate. For the game to be both fun and realistic, you
couldn't allow yourself to cheat at all. I've tried so many times to
recreate that fabulous magical feeling for Lorenzo, but he's
always gone for the PlayStation instead.

"And now," said Giovanni, "I've got to go start studying."

"How come? What time is it over there?"

"Now? It's five o'clock in the evening."

Five meant that Mamma was just about to come home. And
soon she'd prepare tea with cookies, and would set them out on
the table where she would find me studying, convinced that I'd
been there for hours. And that trumped-up break was yet
another happy memory from those days that all too soon would
go into a state of suspended animation.

"What do you all talk about at home these days?"

"Papà is very pleased with his new job and he's making all
sorts of plans; he even daydreams a bit."

This was true; less than two months before his disappearance, Papà had been elected head of the Faculty of Architecture,
and with that, his work had changed a lot.

All this had come about in the wake of a tragic event, which
had left him deeply troubled. Early in the year, a friend of his, a
colleague with whom he'd attended the university and with

whom his early career had been entwined, was killed by terrorists. They'd lain in wait for him on the steps of the Architecture
Faculty, their faces covered by masks, and had shot him point-
blank. I remember the photos of his body lying on the ground,
with chalk marks on the ground indicating the grotesque
position in which he'd landed, and which, now that I think of it,
looked like a funny little person drawn by Keith Haring. I
remember the tragic feeling of that day, with its heavy, loud
pelting of rain, and I remember the moment when Mamma and
Papà returned home that evening. They'd forewarned me,
and I'd followed the news on television. When I opened the
door for them, the man I saw facing me was not the same
person who'd said good-bye to me that morning as I set off for
school. He looked thinner, he had dark shadows under his eyes,
and it looked as if Mamma was holding him up. He hugged me,
walked into the living room, sat down in an armchair, and
started to weep in long, loud sobs. I'd never seen my father
crying, and it had a profound effect on me. I was shocked, and
I locked myself in my room where I then cried as well. I was
crying over my father's tears, though, not over the death of his
friend, whom I didn't know.

The funeral took place a few days later. I saw pictures of it
on TV. There was a huge crowd, and the widow addressed the
terrorists directly, but instead of calling for revenge on them, she
called for them to be pardoned. It struck me as a profound
gesture, as something unthinkable. Children don't have the

right to pardon. They have the duty to apologize and they can only hope to be pardoned.

This is because they don't have, or at least it's said that they don't have, any awareness of right and wrong, of good and evil. There is a secret moment in life in which one passes from the stage of being pardoned to the stage of pardoning, but the Giovanni with whom I was communicating was still far from crossing that threshold. He was about the same age as the daughter of Professor Tessandori, the murder victim. She was the young blonde girl that the TV had furtively framed as she wept during the funeral.

"Giovanni, here's an idea. Don't tell your parents I called, because they don't know that I'm in New York, and when I get back I want to surprise them. How about if I call you again tomorrow? It'll be Saturday, right?"

"Yes, Uncle. But have you lost all track of time in New York?"

"These time-zone changes are very disorienting. So Giovanni, will you do me a favor? Keep a close watch on everything that Papà does, all right? The things he says, the things he wants, whether he seems to be worried or not. All this will help me pick out a good present, which will also be a nice surprise for you."

"Sure, why not? Sounds like fun. Ciao, Uncle Giorgio."

I set the receiver down with infinite slowness. And during that slow motion I realized that I might be on the verge of breaking the incredible spell.

But what if the telephone had turned back into an ordinary one—silent, not magical? What if the chance to speak with a young version of myself had been granted to me only once— just one chance to ride this black bakelite steed across the thirty-year gulf? What if my life were now, once again, swallowed up in bitter waits for dawn and frigid household silences? But I was already a different person from the one who'd gone back and touched the carved tree. I had experienced something inexplicable, something magical and preternatural. I'd been selected, I don't know by whom, to experience this madness, to taste the lack of limits, to experiment with the frontiers lying at infinity. Or perhaps to understand the fact that a gaping hole is capable of generating an immense energy, a power capable of transcending all natural limits. And so here I am, in this empty room, with the sunlight shining on my black bakelite hippogryph. Here I am, with my mind in turmoil and my heart spinning in confusion. Here I am, with a story that cannot be told if one doesn't want to be taken for a fool.

CHAPTER FOUR

I wandered through the house once again, reversing my tracks, checking out every room with fresh eyes and a fresh spirit. Nothing. Just silence, sunlight, the chirping of crickets. Closing the front door behind me, I felt like a rewound film, as if all my motions were mechanically determined. When I finally reached the car, I was all churned up inside.

I put the top down and decided to drive all the way to the sea. Years had passed since I'd done that. And what lured me even more than reaching the sea was the idea of the drive along the way. The city was marvelously deserted. I didn't take the obvious direct route, but instead twisted my way through smaller streets, passing through unfamiliar neighborhoods filled with greenery. Things seemed clearer to me this way, more in focus. And a powerful, inexplicable euphoria flowed through me. So much so that, as I was nearing the sea, I suddenly decided to make a midcourse correction. I swung the car completely around and headed off toward the lake district. Before long, I found myself skirting one of them, and I gazed down at it from above, taking in that special blend of water's blueness and meadows' greenness that always restored serenity to me and made me welcome whatever each day brings me. I parked and set out on foot, soon coming across an isolated little spot under a tree. From it, I surveyed the lake's mirrorlike sheen, and skipped some stones.

Far off, I could make out a tiny girl in a purple T-shirt who was walking perilously close to the water. Something of hers had fallen in, perhaps a game or a doll, and she wanted to retrieve it at all costs. She was making her way down a steep slope with her little feet sideways, while looking back up the hill toward where her parents were sunning themselves; they didn't seem to be aware of her. Repeatedly, she called, went a little further down, then turned around. Meanwhile, the object in the water was being carried further and further away by the current. I started yelling, but I was too far away for anyone to hear me. However, I was pretty sure that the girl stopped, turned, and scanned in my direction with her eyes. But maybe not, for then she continued going down, seeking something to grab hold of. Suddenly, I saw her slip and roll down the slope toward the water, but then she disappeared behind a hedge and I couldn't see where she fell. A moment later, my eyes located a small purplish dot sitting at the lake's edge. By seizing onto the bottom of the hedge, she'd broken her fall, but her legs had wound up in the water. And now that's where she was. On her own, she managed to extricate herself and to sit up straight. But almost as if to protest, she kept her legs in the water and cried, staring at her doll (indeed, that's what it was) now far out in the lake. I was just about to rise, go find her, and console her, but at that moment her parents sat up, took off their headsets, and called their daughter. They ran toward her, but she was annoyed at them and didn't turn around.

I returned to my observation of the lake. I scanned all around it very carefully, eyeballing the distances and taking note of the vegetation. Eventually I grew drowsy and fell fast asleep at the foot of a huge tree. When I woke up, everything was different. The girl with the purple T-shirt was gone, and with her departure no human presence remained. In this spot surrounded by pure, undiluted nature, I was the sole anomaly, and this made me feel ill at ease. I walked back up the slope and found my car.

In the evening, once I was back home, I retired to my attic. When I turned on my computer I found a long email from Lorenzo.

Dear Papà,

I wish I didn't have to write this message, but it's necessary. I've made a big mistake, and now I don't know how to get out of it. I kept a promise made in haste. Stella's here with me, but I can't deal with her any longer. I'm telling you something I have great difficulty even telling myself. What has replaced surprise at seeing these wonderful places is an explosion, every five minutes, of intolerable tantrums. The tiniest thing gets blown up into major proportions: whether or not to go somewhere, whether or not to buy something, whether to put on her pink or her green T-shirt. She seems to do it deliberately, just to drive me up a wall, except then, she'll suddenly start hugging me tightly, for no clear reason. Yesterday, in the trolley car, I was reading and she was seated near me. At some point, out of the blue, she grabbed my book and flipped it away, squeezing me so tightly that I could barely breathe, kissing me, and repeating, "Lorenzo, I love you." And then when we got to our stop, she insisted it was the wrong one and dug in her heels; I couldn't do a thing. I had hoped that this trip would be a thrill for her, but instead it's turning into a nightmare for both of us. There are two things that really hurt me. You know how much I love her, how much I protect her, and try to bring her joy. But surely you also know how much people's stares weigh on me whenever she makes a scene in public. And there's no one I can turn to for help. Something has made her grow colder. It's the remoteness of her sources of security—the two of you, our house—that's rendered her shaky and fragile. And of course, to put it bluntly, I am neither her father nor her mother. Ever since I was eight years old I've been carrying this burden, but this time I took the whole thing on my shoulders alone. Please forgive me if I'm sounding harsh, but this is how things really are. You and Mamma never deprived her of anything, that's certain. The two of you never held back your love. But you do seem to run away from her pains, her shames. You seem to be afraid of her limitations. You seem to disappear at just those key moments when she most needs a big dose of love and support from you. Is it right that I, a twenty-year-old, was the one who had to wash her when she first menstruated? And who had to explain things to her that I barely understand? And who reassured her that it was all right? You can say to me, "But we weren't there at the time." And I could reply, "Par for the course." But that wouldn't be fair, for I know, Papà, how much you do and have done for us. But we need you more than that—take this either as a reproach or as a compliment. And let me add, in this candid letter, that I wouldn't say the same of Mamma.

I've been jealous of your dawns. I've been jealous that they could see you every morning and catch your attention, your thoughts, your emotions. That's why I've sometimes interrupted them with my stories about Marcovaldo and

*Michael Jordan, who might as well be the same person. I
wanted to get you back, just for a little while. And those
talks we had were among the most important events in my
life. Exchanges in which one shares, changes, and grows.
Why do you think my door is always closed? It's because
I'm scared of opening it, scared of your silences, and of the
sounds of the world. You always wondered why I don't read
newspapers and don't watch the news on TV. For one simple
reason: it all frightens me. It reminds me of an oil slick that's
gradually spreading over all of reality. All you ever see are
stories about blood and destruction, hatred and threats. It's a
world without good news. And I don't believe that there's
plenty of good news and someone is merely hiding it. I believe
that we're no longer able to give ourselves good news. We
build gadgets to console ourselves and we get all excited
about trifles while things that truly matter are all going to
hell in a handbasket. In my little room, I have everything
that I live for. And what's missing, I seek elsewhere, in the
outdoors, in people I meet, people I come to like or love, in
the wonders of nature and colors. Aside from that, I have
all I need. These days, I'm only seriously concerned with
great catastrophes, ones that may genuinely change the
course of history and human life. I choose to ignore small oil
slicks spreading toward me. Of course I'd like to stop them,
but I don't know how to. And so I ignore them, opting out of*

the global communications network and building a different one, mine alone. And by the way, Papà, have you noticed that young people of my age live their lives with earphones on? They use them whenever they take even the shortest walk, stroll at night, or meet up together. They don't want to let the times they're living in drive them crazy. Today we've been deprived of every hope that we might share, and we've been shut up in a gleaming supermarket where you can buy anything you want but you can't ever get out.

Stella is not of this world. She has a world of her own that goes more slowly, but every once in a while it grows weird and dangerous. In this city, she feels insecure and so she exaggerates. And sometimes it feels like she's torturing me on purpose. This morning I found her crouching in a corner of our hotel room. Do you remember last summer when her dog got out? Well, today she was crying about that, and was saying that it had been my fault. She knows very well that she was the one who left the front door open. But she's suffered so much that now she can't even accept the blame for something that was entirely her own fault. I just can't handle this anymore. I came here hoping to find a ray of light with which to warm my little Stella, but I've failed and I just can't deal with it any longer. Please, please, come and get her, soon. Much love.

Lorenzo

I can't, my son. You have no idea how much I'd like to, but I simply can't. I can't go away right now. I don't dare interrupt this incredible magic that might possibly carry me back to the very roots of my life, to the days in which the tightrope wire on which we're all walking abruptly snapped.

I can't explain this to him. I can't say a thing to him. I don't want him to think that his father has lost the spark of reason. I wrote him a long answer, but first I sent a message to his mother, who's in Paris now. I told her I couldn't go, that the higher-ups in the Ministry wouldn't let me go. She replied to me with a short and very unexpected message: "Don't worry, I'll go. Lorenzo has done something fantastic. We can't let him do this alone."

The dawn after that astounding day was heavy and gloomy. The television was reporting that in Portugal for the last ten days terrible fires have been devastating the countryside and threatening the cities. The flames have advanced by feeding on the parched vegetation due to a horrific drought, the most serious one in several decades. And the morning's red dawn seemed to contain traces and colors of this conflagration. That night I had troubling dreams. My life passed before my eyes as if it were a film. I was a spectator sitting in an empty movie theater, and every image that I recalled from my earlier life was found precisely in its proper chronological spot. I was the only one, in the movie, who had a blank, featureless face, except at the very end, when, having become a child once again, I was answering the phone. At that point it was me, truly me.

I woke up with a start. I rose and dressed and set off in a hurry, arriving at the country place just as the first rays of light hit it. When I opened the gate I had the impression, no doubt wrong, that there was less disorder, less chaos. I decided that I was just getting used to what had at first surprised me. Then I went inside and wended my way, as usual, back to the phone. I was trembling—trembling from fear that it had all just been a figment of my imagination. I slowly picked up the receiver, sat down on the floor, and dialed the number. It rang, just as it had the day before. "Pronto?" said a little voice once again, and hardly ever have I known as much joy in a reunion with anyone.

"Pronto, Giovanni, it's your Uncle."

"Ciao, Uncle, how are you?"

"Good. What time is it where you are?"

"It's ten in the evening."

"Oh, so Mamma and Papà are at home?"

"No, they went out to dinner. It was a very scary day, you know…"

"What happened?"

"All day long here in the center of town there have been terrible clashes between demonstrators and the police. There have been bloody beatings, and we also heard gunshots."

"And where was Papà all this time?"

"He was here with me. We watched it all from our window. You wouldn't believe how much confusion there's been—all the sirens, all the ambulances. Every so often we would open the windows to get a better view, but we couldn't leave them open for long because of the tear gas. We all had red eyes. At one point we saw some young people with ski masks completely covering their faces jump some unlucky policeman, and they started bashing him over and over again with a wooden club. The poor fellow tried to shield his face, but then they kicked him, and when they finally took off, he was just lying there unconscious, beside a big garbage bin. Papà and I didn't know what to do. We certainly couldn't call the police. Every so often the demonstrators would set fire to a car and huge red flames would soar skywards. You could hear screams of fear and pain. It lasted for hours, never seeming to end. I was scared to death. On TV they said that an armory had been plundered and lots of guns were stolen. Tell me, Uncle Giorgio—what's going on?"

"What's going on, Giovanni, is that smashing heads is easier than thinking. It's easier to destroy than to build. But how did Papà react to all this?"

"He didn't react; he didn't say a word. At one point I turned around when we were at the window, and there was something strange about him. His face was lit up by the fire, but his gaze was lowered. He wasn't looking; he seemed absent. He said a couple of words, something like 'It's all madness,' and then he went back to his desk. He works so hard, you know? And he seems very satisfied. Ever since he's been head of the Architecture Faculty, he's had a whole lot more to do. And many more projects are on the boards in his studio. In fact, I even heard Mamma and Papà making plans to buy a larger house and a new car."

Good God, how can I tell him that all these things that seem to be going so well will no longer exist in twenty-four hours? How can I tell him that there's only one day left until all his dreams go poof and the great vacuum takes over? Or can I find some way to prevent all that from happening? Can I, working from here, modify history, intervene in the course of events? Can the magic that I'm experiencing somehow change destiny? Actually, that's already happened.

Giovanni had to answer the telephone because I called him, from thirty years away in the future. And he got up and went to fetch a newspaper. That is, he did something that depended on a desire that was born *here*, in this abandoned house, nearly thirty years later. Something that I myself *didn't* do, that day. Or at least that I don't recall having done. How can I keep him from waking up tomorrow morning and finding Papà gone? But then again, even if I could keep Papà from running away tomorrow, who could prevent it from happening the next day? And even if it never took place, how would that affect my life today? Where would Papà be? And what would have happened to me? The incredible dream that I'm having right now shouldn't allow me, *must* not allow me, to change the course of events in the past—unless it simply reveals the meaning or the reasons behind the actual events.

But there's no revelation that could help me soothe the anguish of that young boy, an anguish that I know only too well. There would be no sense in trying to prepare him for what's coming. So instead I just say, "Giovanni, tomorrow is Sunday, isn't it?"

"Yes, Uncle."

"Well then, why don't you do the following? This evening go get into the big bed in your parents' room. You'll see that Mamma and Papà are pleased with the surprise. And tomorrow morning, wake up early and *you* be the one to fix breakfast. And then stay with Papà all day long. He'll like that, you'll see."

"All right, Uncle. Will you call me tomorrow?"

"Of course I will, Giovanni."

CHAPTER FIVE

What did I do that morning? I did indeed sleep in my parents' bed, but I woke up late, very late. We'd been planning to go see the soccer game. What I liked best, on such occasions, was the hastily eaten lunch—wolfed down almost while standing up. This gave me the sense that something so grand was in the offing that even eating was a waste of time. Then there was the excitement of the wait. To me it didn't really matter if the game actually took place. What mattered was just the thrilling feeling of seeing that great green field and those thousands of colors. The most intense moment was when we would climb the stairs that led to the grandstands. You'd start to hear the roar of the crowd, and, bit by bit, step by step, all that green would start to appear. Each time I reached the top of the stairs, I'd be so excited I could barely breathe. The feeling was all the more powerful because, back in those days of my youth, the soccer fields on TV were always black and white and the fans were just various shades of gray. But this green was the real thing, incomparably more beautiful than its image on the screen.

My first thought that morning was of the game. I got out of bed and looked for Mamma and Papà. They weren't in the dining room, but on the table there were a couple of newspapers whose pages were being wildly whipped about by a chilly wind coming in through a wide-open window. There was no one at home. It struck me as strange, even though I remembered Mamma having said that, in the morning, she'd be going to my grandmother's to take her to mass. But where was Papà? Wouldn't we be late for the match?

I quickly threw some breakfast together and then began reading a comic book. But all the while I was getting more and more impatient, and I started to do something that children don't do—I started counting the minutes. I watched the clock, thinking about each thing that we'd have to do before we could leave. Children don't have a sense of time, or at least they aren't victims of its harsh rule. There's an African saying about the frenzy of Westerners' lives that runs: "You've got clocks but we've got time." And children could say it just as easily.

But that was the day I started to understand the anxiety that flows from time. In that empty house, with my heart filled with anticipation, the clock hands were zooming around like racecars.

I heard the sound of keys in the lock and things started looking up. But it was just Mamma returning.

"What about Papà?" I asked.

"Isn't he home?" she replied with surprise. And as she was taking off her overcoat, she began, almost mechanically, to wander through the various rooms as if she really imagined that I'd somehow failed to see him. Once she reached the dining room, she closed the window and said, "When I went out this morning he was reading the papers. He'd gone out early to buy them and then he came back. But he knew he had to go to the stadium with you. He must have had to go somewhere. I won't even ask you if anyone phoned because you're one who could sleep through cannons firing. Let's wait a bit; he'll let us know where he is."

"Yes, Mamma, but the match is going to start soon and if we wait much longer we won't ever get there in time."

"Your father isn't irresponsible. He's very aware that he made this date with you. He'll be back in time. Or else, if something came up, he'll give us a call—don't worry."

But I wasn't in the least calm. In fact, I was very ticked off at Papà, because he was letting me down on one of the few occasions that we had a chance to do something together, just the two of us. I'd gotten all dressed up and was sitting in the front hall with my overcoat right by me. I was thinking that I might have to dash down the stairs, so I should be all ready.

In the meantime, Mamma was tidying up the house. I heard her exclaim to herself, "How odd—the suitcase is missing." Then I could hear her worriedly opening the drawers in the closet. I got up and went in, finding her extremely disturbed.

"His shirts and sweaters are gone, and so is his underwear. Did you run across a note anywhere? Go look and see if you can't find some little written note somewhere."

I started going through the house, but I didn't turn up a thing. The only trace of his presence was the newspapers; otherwise nothing at all. As she sat down on the bed, my mother said, "Maybe he had to go out in a hurry. You'll see, he'll call us as soon as he finds a public telephone." But hours passed. Mamma started calling friends and relatives. And she kept on saying into the phone that really, nothing much could have happened, that the missing suitcase clearly proved he'd taken off because he'd been suddenly called away on business, and that we just needed to be patient. By saying this to others, she reassured herself. She did her best, that Sunday, to project calmness, but it was all playacting. She asked me questions about school and my friends. I answered, but I could see that her gaze was elsewhere. She even voiced interest, through an amazing effort of emotional transfer, in how the soccer game was going, since I was watching it on a small television set.

I very much enjoyed that way of experiencing soccer—much more than on the radio. In fact, what dominated the screen, in televised soccer games, was a big white ball that lit up whenever anyone made a goal. And the moment between the ball's bright flash and the announcement down on the field that the score had changed always gave me a big thrill. But that day in our house, everything felt fake, including my excitement. As time wore on, the house slowly started to fill up with grandparents, relatives, and friends. Mamma tried to find Uncle Giorgio, but he turned out to be on a trip in some faraway country. One of Papà's work colleagues phoned the hospitals and also called a friend of his who worked at a newspaper. But nothing of note had happened involving Professor Astengo, Giacomo Astengo. This piece of news was a bit reassuring, but also somewhat worrisome. Yes, nothing had happened, but he had nonetheless disappeared. There didn't seem to be any suddenly announced Sunday meetings on architecture, nor any meetings of the Faculty Council. What could possibly have made him bolt out of the house? And especially without leaving a note or anything at all? Everything hung on a telephone call, everything was tied to the chance that the black bakelite phone would ring, and that Professor Astengo, at the other end, would furnish a clear explanation, or at least *some* kind of explanation. And thus time ticked by all day. Each visitor had a guess, an idea. Everyone was part psychologist and part detective. One guest came out with a sentence that he claimed explained the whole thing. My mother, trying to keep herself from facing the truth, made a big fuss in the kitchen, offering everyone tea, coffee, and pastries. It felt like a sad party for a friend who'd vanished into thin air. But it was much sadder than it was festive.

In the evening, just as everyone was about to go home, the black bakelite telephone rang, as it had so often in these tense hours. But this moment seemed different, with the day coming to an end. And in fact it *was* different. Mamma answered and her face went ashen. Everyone was huddled around her, but she motioned them all away with a gesture of her hand. And so the crowd of well-meaning friends, just as it had collected in silence around the telephone, now broke up into streams of chatter in the various rooms of the house. I didn't know what I should do—consider myself one of the herd to be scattered, or live up to my filial role and stay close to Mamma? I chose the latter, but it was a mistake. She waved me away as well, then stroked my head to soften the blow, but I got her message that I had to clear out. I've never forgotten that moment and the anguish I felt. I went back to my room, but found it full of jabbering people, so then I shut myself into the bathroom. It struck me that if the house had been roofless and someone hovering high above had been able to gaze down on it, everything would have been clear.

They would have seen a woman on the phone waiting to find out what was in store for her for the rest of her life. Dozens of people eating pastries and making comments on personal matters in this already shattered family. A buzzing anthill of words that were useless and in fact indifferent to the tragedy that was taking place. And there, in the bathroom, a young boy sitting on the bidet, with his hands covering his eyes, waiting, sobbing, feeling abandoned, and now even excluded. This is how it was in my house on the evening of March 13, 1977.

When the call was over, my mother summoned everyone into the living room. As I could tell that silence had fallen, I emerged from my hiding place, not waiting for anyone to come and get me, partly out of fear that no one would do so. My mother was standing up in front of everyone. She had to say something but she didn't want to say anything. All she said was, "It was Giacomo. He's fine, nothing happened. He just needs to be alone for a while—to travel a bit. He'll be back soon and he sends you all his greetings. And now, please excuse me . . ."

The colorful herd started breaking up, gathering overcoats and umbrellas, and one by one heading for the door. There were many strange remarks and everyone was taking great care, like vaudeville actors exiting the stage, to leave Mamma with some reassuring message, each time accompanied by the unbearable refrain of "I told you nothing had happened." I hated them. Once they'd left, they would go to a movie or a pizzeria or their home, to rejoin their children. But after the door had closed behind the last of the stragglers, Mamma and I remained alone. Truly alone. The house seemed huge, partly because of the emptiness, partly because of the silence. Once again, if someone hovering high above had gazed down on it, they would have seen the walls growing a thousand times higher, the ceilings soaring far into the sky, the rooms moving apart from each other, separated by immensely long corridors. Mamma held my hand. And she said to me, "Don't be worried, Giovanni." Aside from the fact that I'd never heard a mother say to her child "be worried," this just seemed a bit too feeble, given what was taking place. I lost my patience, and to make it clear, I removed my hand from hers. But she pursued my hand on the table and then answered my irritated question, "Can't you tell me what Papà said to you?"

"He just said he's tired, a bit exhausted. That he's been working too hard these past few months and needs some rest. He needs a bit of silence, needs to sleep, needs not to worry about anything."

"So he needs all these things, but not *us*?"

"It's not like that, Giovanni. It's just that in life this kind of thing can happen. A person can simply want to be alone for a while. Sometimes you're just tired of everyone, even the people you love the most. Sometimes you just need peace and quiet."

"I'm only thirteen years old. Are people already growing tired of me? Especially my own father?"

"It can happen, sweetheart. But in these kinds of situations, you have to open up your heart to those you love. You have to accept things you don't think of as right. You have to be able to wait, with hope."

"You mean that although *he* wasn't willing to do that, *we* have to do it?"

"No, Giovanni, we have to do what he wasn't *able* to do."

In short, we would have to be better people than my father. At this point, that didn't strike me as very hard. I asked her point-blank, "Did he ask about me?"

For a split second, her eyes betrayed her, showing my question had caught her off guard. But quickly she pulled herself together and said, "Yes, of course he did. He told me to give you a big hug and to tell you that he's thinking about you." But that split second was too obvious; it had been too long and too intense. Mamma had been forced to lie, and perhaps to experience a double dose of shame. First, for her husband, who had taken off without leaving a single word for his child, and second, for herself, for not having thought to ask him what she should say to me.

That night I slept once again in my parents' big bed. But it, too, had grown larger, along with everything else in the house. It felt immense, during the night. My first night as a fatherless child.

CHAPTER SIX

Yesterday there was a mad dash toward dawn. I could barely wait, while I was asleep, for morning to come. Basile would have put it this way: "Not a moment too soon did the Sun, with its butcher's-broom of rays, brush away the dreary soot of Night...." Yes, not a moment too soon did the dawn come, that August day. But when it came, it was so memorable. I saw every color in the world, a panoply of marvels. I witnessed the power of change, the transition that turns dawn into daylight and concludes, day after day, in well-deserved glory. For that special day there was a special dawn. And I found a short email message from Lorenzo that said, "Is Mamma really coming? I can't believe it, but I'm very glad. Stella's behaving worse and worse. Too bad the night of San Lorenzo [August 10] is already past. Just kidding. But really, I could strangle her. I need to be alone for a while. Ciao." All this was fine, except for that last sentiment, which bothered me.

The top image on the Web site for the news today shows a mother carrying the mutilated body of a dead child in her arms. I didn't notice what country this had taken place in, or if the child was a victim of terrorism or of an act of war.

I was also struck by a news item on the Web site of the journal *Science*. A group of German researchers has discovered that icebergs sing—or more precisely, that "the water that penetrates the crevices under high pressure makes them sing." And I imagine, now that the crevices are widening as a result of global warming, that their song will grow ever more intense and anguished—a swan song heralding the iceberg's breakup and its subsequent melting into the great ocean. It makes me think of the pieces of music composed by prisoners in concentration camps.

By now the dawn is over and I can return to my tasks. The garden is really lovely today. Maybe I'm just getting used to it, but I truly feel that there are fewer brambles than before, and that the tree on which we carved our heights is less bent over by its heavy branches. The telephone beckons. With its own brilliant sunrise, it awaits me. And so now I'll call myself. I've just realized that the time travel I indulge in whenever I dial that number carries me to the next day, exactly thirty years ago, after my previous phone call. But the hour, on the other hand, is unpredictable. My impossible communication link has a temporal randomness.

I'm very frightened of making today's call. I might burst in right at the moment when the big crowd was in the house and everyone was talking. Or perhaps in the morning, when people had just found out what had happened. And each ring of the phone, that day back then, seemed to be a siren that held out some hope of a rescue.

I tried. Halfway through the number, I heard a noise and saw a cat in the hallway. It stopped for a moment, right in front of the doorway. Stock still, it fixed its yellow eyes on me. We looked at each other, motionless, for several seconds. Here were endlessly tumbling dust particles, a great silence, a black bakelite telephone, an impish cat, and an archivist of diaries. All of them frozen in time, like a memory. Then the cat resumed its ambling and I finished dialing my number.

Someone picked up after the very first ring. It was Giovanni—it was I myself. I heard an agitated and confused voice say, "Pronto?"

"Giovanni, it's me," I began, and followed with the most cruel of questions, "How are you?"

"Uncle, something strange happened . . . " His voice was trembling. He was all alone at home in the presence of a mystery, and this made him more serious but also more helpless.

Apparently my call had come just a few moments before Mamma would get back. Giovanni told me about everything: the soccer match, my father's promise to take me to it, the inexplicably empty bed, the newspapers, the open window. He also told me something I didn't recall—namely, that he'd even gone and stared out the window, pushed by a strange sense of foreboding. "This isn't Papà's normal behavior, is it?"

Given what little I knew at that point, I really didn't know what to say. I tried to calm him down, but not too much. And that was the precise moment when I decided to start seeking answers to all my questions, using myself as a child as my conduit. I would search for the reasons behind the disappearance of Giacomo Astengo, architect.

I said to Giovanni, "Let's be calm. Mamma will be back in a moment. It might be that Papà had to go out and so he'll come back soon, or perhaps he just had something urgent to take care of. There has to be some reason, and maybe he just didn't have the time to tell anyone. Let's take things systematically. Go into their bedroom and look on his night table. What do you find?"

"Wait a minute. Okay, I've got it. Just a book."

"What book?"

"Andersen's fairy tales."

"Well, is there anything inside it—a piece of paper, a note, something underlined?"

"No, I don't think so. Or rather, yes. There's a bookmark in it."

"What page?"

"At the start of a story called 'The Shadow.'"

"All right. Now go and try something forbidden for me. Go check in the pockets of Papà's jackets and pants to see if there are any slips of paper, receipts for train trips or plane trips, or anything else at all."

"All right. Hold on for a moment."

Some time passed and Giovanni came back. I had the impression that his sadness and fear were being replaced by a curiosity about our quest, by a quiver of excitement at making these intrusions. And that he clearly felt reassured by the concern of his uncle in America, so far away—in fact, thirty years away. He came back to the phone and said, "Yes, there were some things, Uncle. But something else just struck me."

"Tell me."

"A few jackets are gone—at least three. For example, the blue one is missing, and so is the beige one with the leather patches on the elbows, and then his overcoat and his raincoat, as well. He couldn't possibly have put them all on . . . "

"Well, that means it's very likely that he had to leave on a trip. Anyway, what did you find?"

"A movie ticket, some photocopies of a receipt for a restaurant a couple of months ago, some little notes written by colleagues or maybe students."

"What do the little scraps of paper say?"

"Let's see . . . One's a teaching schedule showing days, times, and places. Another is a library notice for some book on architecture, then there are various little notes from the Architecture Faculty library. Oh, there's also an invitation to a conference a couple of months ago. And there's even Papà's name, among the speakers."

"All right, Giovanni. Do something for me. Put all these things in a drawer. For the time being they aren't of much use, but hold on to them anyway. And by the way, Giovanni, don't tell anyone that we're having these conversations. I'll let you in on a secret: I came to America because of a woman, but I don't want anyone to know about it. It's an adult secret, so will you keep it?"

"Of course, Uncle, trust me. Do you . . . Do you think that Papà also could have gone away because of some woman?"

That question devastated me. Recalling my timidity back in those days, I thought about how much pain, loneliness, and confusion it must have taken to transmit this question all the way from brain to tongue, via the heart.

"Uncle, I have to go now. I hear the keys turning in the lock. Probably it's Mamma." As he was putting the receiver down, I heard him shout out "Mamma" with an intonation that conveyed a sense of deep worry.

The rest of the story I know only too well. I know all about that afternoon and evening. In order to think things through I stayed in the empty house, just wandering here and there. Every so often I would spin around because I seemed to hear the voices of children playing happily somewhere. But God only knows where that was coming from. I thought about what other kinds of information I might try to extract from myself, on that fateful day. And I realized I hadn't asked him anything about the newspapers. It occurred to me that I could easily get copies of that day's papers in a library, maybe even on the Web. But which ones would my father have read that morning? Would he have made notes in the margins, the way he so often did? Could I wait till tomorrow? And what if they'd already thrown the papers away?

Screwing up my courage, I decided to call once again. But what juncture would I land at, this time? In the middle of the night? Before or after Papà's phone call? And all those guests—where were the chattering guests? I couldn't lose a moment. I dialed the number once again, ready to hang up if I heard a voice that didn't belong, so to speak. But once again, I hit the target—I myself answered. I only let Giovanni say "Pronto" and then, without losing a beat, I asked him, "What's going on at home right now?"

"A lot of friends are here."

"And Mamma?"

"She's in there with them." I heard him yelling in the direction of the dining room, "No, Mamma—just a classmate calling about homework." Back then, I certainly knew how to keep a secret—I did it well. Then he added, still addressing his mother, "Yes, I'll just be a second, don't worry."

I said to him, "Giovanni, don't throw away the newspapers; put them away with those other papers. And tomorrow morning, say you've got a bit of a fever and try not to go to school."

"But how can I do that? Tomorrow I have to turn in an assignment in Italian class."

"Don't worry about that. Didn't you just get a '10'? Surely they'll give you a final grade of at least '8.'"

"How would you know?"

"I'm just guessing, but also I have a lot of faith in you. I'll call you tomorrow."

"All right, I'll do my best."

At school I was a good student, especially in subjects having to do with literature. I felt enormous admiration for Giacomo Leopardi, and this has never left me. And even way back then, I was fascinated by diaries. Those of writers, where real life and pure flights of fancy were intimately blended together, and where, very often, life and fiction were blurred, like reality and dreams. In this way their diaries became new planets, artificial realms in which real and invented people, flesh and fantasy, coexisted side by side.

It may well be that my having lived so many vicarious lives is the reason I'm the one to whom this amazing, magical thing is happening. Almost an award of merit. As if to say, "You've done what one should do. You've stepped out of yourself. You've stopped seeing time and life as a road to travel from the first mile to the last, merely waiting for it to end. You've understood that life should be lived with the strength that comes from curiosity. That one has to follow not only grand tree-lined boulevards but also dirt roads, which carry one far from the obvious paths. That one has to explore these pathways, come to know them, and internalize them. Because in that way, life's journey is longer and much richer. Whoever does this will be rewarded. I will allow you to do forbidden things, to go down pathways in the wrong direction, to revisit what you've already visited, and to understand it more clearly, enriched by a deeper awareness of the landscape and its byways, leading off in every direction and inviting you to explore them. As long as you do this, you will not arrive deprived of speech after crossing the forest. All you will need is your experience in order to tell your tales and to listen."

This is what has been granted to me. Or else I've granted it to myself. I've learned, or am learning, how to use reverse gear. This reminds me of a present that Lorenzo gave me at Christmas. It's a computer printout with a big figure from a tarot card showing a man hanging upside down. Underneath the picture there's a quote from Lorenzo's dear Calvino: "Leave me like this. I've been everywhere and I've learned. The world has to be read in reverse. Now I get it!" Ever since, I've kept that poster in plain sight on a wall in the attic, held up by a yellow thumbtack. It's one of my faithful comrades at dawn. Often we get together—the poster, the monsters in my silent TV set, and I—to contemplate how fast time flies. Yesterday I saw some strange and disturbing images on the screen. There were fat children in Disneyland, and superimposed on them were statistical tables showing that the percentage of obese teenagers in America has quintupled in the last twenty years. Right after that, they showed a photo of a tiny gray heart stuck onto the pupil of someone's eye. This was certainly odd—an ocular piercing. Later, I found out that it had been dreamt up in some advertising campaign for the Netherlands Institute for Innovative Ocular Surgery, offering you a choice of tiny jewels to implant in your iris.

I read a diary one time, the diary of a man into whose body was implanted not a little smiley-faced heart but a real heart and kidney. It told of his yearning to find out about the life of the donor, and also about the donor's death. The book told the story of the author's illness, the long wait, the operation, and the rebirth. But it was also a story written in reverse order: a donation, a death, an accident, a life. And also the story of a friendship nourished, day in and day out, by the steady beating of a shared heart.

I went to dinner all alone in a restaurant, one of the few that are open during the mid-August holidays in this city. I found one in a lively part of town. It's in a *piazza*, and people gather there each evening as if they'd all just come back outside after an air-raid alarm. At sunset the men and women come down from their apartments, often carrying a chair with them. They sit down, making little shifting groups that shrink or grow, depending on the topic of conversation. And people tell stories—adventures that have befallen them, ideas they've had. As their words and thoughts flow, they get more and more worked up. And they take turns speaking and listening. Every so often someone sticks their head out a window one floor up and peers down. It's almost always a man in an undershirt with a few days' growth of beard. You can see the television flashing away in his room. And the guy always chimes in with some remark. He's a kind of sentinel posted up there to monitor the world around him. There are basically just two types of news items that he cares about: disasters and sports. From my table I can see one of these fellows popping his head out the window. Now he's peering down, watching the group of people seated right below him. He carefully waits for his chance to jump in and then blurts out, "Did you hear the news? Some plane ran out of fuel in midair and crashed. What a bunch of idiots." It's like throwing fish into a school of sharks. This little news item launches a whole new wave of talk—everyone has their own tale to tell. Most of the time the stories are just hearsay because the folks sitting in the local *piazza* on a mid-August evening have led very limited, provincial lives. One older lady declares that one time one of her daughter's co-workers did such-and-so . . . and adds that some acquaintance of hers talked with somebody who works at Alitalia . . . It's really wonderful to see all this happening, especially to see it still happening today. To hear peoples' voices mingling, to see them so eager to talk together, to know they feel such a need for company and for exchanging stories.

When I got home I remembered, shortly before falling asleep, how the poster of the black athletes had come to be at our country house. It was in fact Uncle Giorgio who'd given it to us right after returning from New York by plane. And as he handed it to me, he'd told me, with a very proud tone, "Always remember that in life you only need to do one thing: Stand up straight." Those words have stuck with me ever since. And they've inspired deep respect in me for two types of people—those who have principles, and those who are on their way out. Or, more precisely, those who stick to their principles even when the going gets risky or dangerous, and those who dismount from their horse with dignity, without protesting, without shouting. The first type I've encountered in many books, and also in many of my diaries. Some of them merely claimed to have principles; they were the worst. But others had truly followed a path of denial so as not to betray their own values.

There was a time—in fact, not just one—when everyone said yes. But at some point someone very simply said, "I would rather not." I admire such small acts of courage, the kind that are found on the front lines of battle, where lives are risked and lost. Acts that are like closing a door forever behind oneself, acts undertaken solely out of principle. During the Fascist regime there were twelve professors who had the courage to refuse to take the loyalty oath. They did this without any show, with unassuming simplicity. One of them in particular had a huge impact on me. This was Professor Bartolo Nigrisoli, who held the chair of surgery at the University of Bologna. He had already declined the nomination to senatorship that had been enthusiastically proposed by a Monsignor in the Church, saying, "Please take my name off the list; I don't wish to have any part in this honor for a number of reasons: in part, because I do not deserve it, but also because my beliefs are in total opposition to all that it represents." But the gesture that I most admired of his was another. The day on which the Faculty of Medicine was abuzz with the news that Professor Nigrisoli had refused to sign the loyalty oath and had consequently been removed from his chair, he came into the large classroom. There he was received with a courageous ovation from students and teachers, which he cut short, requesting them to "Stop immediately, for otherwise I will walk out this instant and will never return."

A simple "no." A willingness to give up everything in order to preserve an invisible link with one's own core values.

The second type, those who are leaving the stage, I've often run into in real life. One time at the Ministry, for instance, when a new director general was named, all my thoughts and emotions were focused on the person who was being replaced and was retiring. And while everyone was rushing up to congratulate and fawn over the new symbol of power, I carefully followed the way in which the departing figure's office was being emptied out. I was somehow drawn to the melancholy of these moments. There were those who would cart everything off, packed up in boxes that would allow them to keep dreaming of all sorts of future activities, although most of the time the boxes were just relegated to the basement forever. Then there were those who only took away their personal effects. And they would usually start doing so very early, very discreetly. And thus, the final day, all they had to do was slip their pen, very slowly, into their vest pocket, and then close the door for one last time. The worst moments, though, were the retirement parties, always featuring fancy watches and the inevitable poem written and read aloud by some co-worker. The atmosphere of fake jollity on such occasions greatly troubled me. I preferred to wait by the door for the departing ones, and to say to them, quite simply, "Thank you for all you've done." The reaction would just be a sad smile. Yes, but at least a sincere one. And I would stay to watch the departing ones set off for their cars. To me it felt as if I was watching a fade-out in the movie of each person's life, and in a very small way, in the life of everyone.

I saw that poster again the next day. I'd arrived early in the morning and I'd started to clean up a bit in the garden. In the house I had run across a pair of shears and was using them to try to prune the bushes back. I removed all the dry leaves and tore out all the weeds that had invaded the meadow. It was very tiring work. And when I went back inside, I was all sweaty and beet red. But the greenery outside, when seen from the darkness of the rooms inside, now seemed even more brilliant and vivid, and I was very pleased with my handiwork. I waited until I caught my breath and could concentrate again, and then I called the Astengo home. The same boy answered and told me everything that had happened the night before, exactly as I remembered it, using the very words that were etched into my memory. Then he told me that he'd feigned a severe stomachache, and that Mamma, who put his malady down to a large gelato he'd eaten the day before, had left to go to work and then to meet a colleague of Papà's at lunchtime.

I asked him whether he'd kept the newspapers. He said yes, he had them right there. He read me the headlines, the subheads, and the summaries: "Gunfights and fires, two armories sacked, newspaper offices attacked. Dozens wounded. Interior Minister proclaims: 'No more appeasing of the Tupamaros.'" In the middle of the page it said: "Bologna still in turmoil. Inquest on the death of the student Lorusso. More troubles at the university." And at the bottom: "Giuseppe Ciotta murdered. Police representative assassinated like Calabresi."

I asked him to check the other pages, to see if there were any notes jotted in the margins. He read me the headlines, saw that Papà hadn't written himself any notes. There didn't seem to be anything important—that is, not until Giovanni said, "Wait, Uncle, maybe this . . ."

"Maybe what?"

"There's a short article a few pages in, which has to do with the killing of Professor Tessandori."

"Okay, read it to me."

The headline and subhead stated: "Murderers of the Dean of Architecture arrested. Brigade members were preparing another attack." And in the article it said that the investigators had cracked the case, thanks to a series of depositions of students in the Architecture Faculty. And in the terrorists' secret hideout, plans to hit again in the same place had been found. Just a few lines, a short mention of the ongoing investigation of the murder, nothing more.

"Well, it's the only news item that might be of help to us, one way or another."

In fact, for Papà, the death of his best friend had been a genuine tragedy. They'd grown up together, they used to go on vacations together. They'd graduated from the university in the same year, and they'd won national competitions for professorships in the same year. When Tessandori died, Papà always spoke of these two parallel lives. Tessandori had been chosen over Papà as Dean of the Faculty, and they'd celebrated the event together. When he was killed, it struck everyone as only natural that Papà should take his place, but Papà was heartsick at the thought of doing so. He was truly devastated by this murder committed in such a heinous fashion in the very place where they both had grown up, worked, and lived. One evening, some time after Papà's nomination, when I was going to get a glass of water in the kitchen, I heard him cry out in fear to Mamma, "Do you think it will happen to me, too?" I understood that they were speaking of the murder of Tessandori. And in fact, for the first few months Papà always had a police escort. After a while, the situation returned to an appearance of normalcy.

Papà organized a commemorative ceremony in the Architecture Faculty, scheduled to take place exactly one month after Tessandori's death. And he made a point of asking me to come to it. And so I wound up sitting next to a girl of my own age, that same girl whom I'd seen crying on television. And now, with heavy heart and a new sense of responsibility, she was listening carefully, but with dry eyes, to *my* father's eulogy for *her* father. And we, the children, were sitting side by side. She had greeted me in a polite fashion and had asked me my age. I replied but was embarrassed, not having the foggiest idea of what to say in a situation of this sort. I mumbled something like, "I'm very sorry." And she replied, "Me too." Her words troubled me. I couldn't tell if they were a snide reaction to my ill-prepared remark or an innocently straightforward reply. She had big blue eyes, and from time to time I glanced at her out of the corner of my eye. At the end of the ceremony she said to me, "Your father gave a very good talk. Please thank him." "Thank *you*" was the only thing that came out of my mouth.

On that day, the main reading room in the Architecture Faculty's library was renamed in memory of Tessandori. It was a large hall full of books and magazines, and it looked directly onto the main entrance to the university. The girl pointed out a spot halfway between the large gate of the library and the corner of the street and said to me, "That's the place where they killed my father." Her intonation was shaky, so it wasn't clear to me whether she was stating a fact or asking a question. Just to cover myself, I nodded my head. Then her mother embraced her tightly, and they both looked down on that spot to which, each day, a few people would still bring bouquets of flowers.

I asked Giovanni to see if the date of the murder was mentioned in the article. He checked very carefully and answered, "Yes. Here's what it says: 'The murder of Professor Tessandori was carried out on January 15 just after the end of morning classes, at around 1:30 p.m. The Dean of Architecture was killed by a commando made up of three people, two men and a woman, who were lying in wait for him at the main door of the Faculty. He had taken a few steps toward the street corner when the woman, who was following him, called his name. He turned around and was hit in the chest by several bullets. The three murderers fled on foot and managed to get away.'"

The fifteenth of January. "How did the memorial service for Tessandori go, Giovanni?"

"It was sad. I was very moved by the daughter. She looked extremely sad. And yet she didn't cry. She listened to Papà very carefully, and at the end she even clapped for a long time. There were so many professors and students."

"Where did you all go after the memorial service?"

"First they held the dedication ceremony for the main room

of the Library, and after that we went out to lunch with a group of Papà's colleagues."

"Giovanni, do you still have those slips of paper that you found in Papà's pockets?"

"Yes, right here, next to the newspapers. Just as you wanted."

"Okay—let's go over them together."

"All right. One is the schedule of classes for the first trimester."

"Is it Papà's schedule, or someone else's?"

"Well, it says 'Schedule of Professor Giacomo Astengo.'"

"Fine. And then?"

"Then there's a photocopy of a movie ticket, but the name of the theater isn't on it. And then there's one last photocopy—just some restaurant bill."

"He probably got himself reimbursed for various things, though I doubt that the university covers movie outings. What restaurant is it?"

"The one just below his office, where we went on the day of the ceremony."

"Maybe it's even the receipt for that day."

"Let me see… No, just for one meal. And anyway, it's for January 15."

"That's the day Tessandori was killed."

"Oh, right. Maybe he kept it to remember the day."

"Yeah, to remember it. And what about the notices for the library books?"

"There are so many, Uncle. Do you want me to read you the names of the books?"

"No, just tell me the dates."

"Well, let's see . . . There are about ten of them. They start in the middle of November and run to mid-February."

"Check to see if there's one dated January 15."

"No, there's not, Uncle. But why?"

"To find out whether he kept *everything* connected with that day as a memory. Giovanni, do you recollect anything from these past weeks, anything peculiar that happened to Papà, or anything strange at home?"

"No, I don't think so. Well, one time Papà came home very shaken. Since he was a friend of Tessandori, he'd been interrogated by the police. When he got back, he told Mamma that they'd asked him whether Tessandori had any enemies in the Architecture Faculty or if Papà was aware of terrorist cells at the university. I remember him saying to Mamma that they'd asked him a lot of questions about a certain graduate assistant. He was surprised by that, because this person struck him as an outstanding fellow, someone who would never harm anyone. But otherwise, no, I don't recall anything unusual."

I'd always thought that my father was frightened that he might be killed. And now I remember that one of his colleagues was suspected by the police of having plotted the murder of his best friend. Could this have been the reason for my father's taking off? Was he terrified by that uncontrollable, irrational feeling called fear? Did he leave, in those terrible years, because he was frightened for his life? Or else maybe even for *our* lives? In which case, his act of cowardice could in fact be quite the opposite. Maybe he gave up everything in order to save us. But then, when things were no longer chaotic, why didn't he ever return? God only knows what thoughts occur to a man who is far from home, frightened, and on the run. A man who is forced to run away not because he's been exiled, not because he's an enemy of law and order, but simply because pitiless forces of terrorism, hell-bent on revenge, are relentlessly hunting him down. There are judges who have been killed as many as four or five years after having sentenced Red Brigade members. And police officers who have been tracked for years, with their deaths announced in advance and sworn to in blood. My father might well have thought that his number was up, that the shooters who killed Tessandori had internal connections in the Faculty, and that they could easily now have *him* in their crosshairs.

All at once, Giovanni recalled one other fact. And only now did he ascribe any importance to it. Papà had insisted on opening all the mail himself, and moreover, if he was at home, he insisted on being the only one ever to answer the phone.

"This evening, would you ask Mamma why he did this? It's important."

Giovanni was sounding ever more lost and frightened. I well recall those first few hours. It's just that these days I no longer know if the acts that I'm making myself-as-child perform—the rifling of pockets, the searching of newspapers, not to mention answering all my questions that trigger memories and further questions in his young mind—truly belong to a period that I genuinely lived through.

"I've got to go now, Giovanni. Please don't forget to ask Mamma that question. But try to stay very calm. Things will work out. It won't be easy, but they'll work out, trust me."

I heard a long silence and then a few words in an unnatural tone. "All right, Uncle. All right," he said in a soft little voice that I didn't recognize.

"Do you feel like crying? Then cry."

I don't think he could have done anything else. He burst out in loud sobs, and then I, too, joined in. I could so easily picture him in that old house that I knew so well—big, empty, and silent. His tears must have made a loud noise, almost embarrassing. And this was not the type of crying that provides relief. It was a primordial outpouring, a flow of tears because something terrible was just starting up, not because something terrible was ending. I let him cry those tears of mine while consoling him but never overdoing it.

At that point I would so much have liked to reveal everything to him, to tell him about the black bakelite phone in the *casa del sertão*. But he would have thought I was a madman. I had no way to prove to him that I wasn't a crackpot. I knew things his future whose plausibility would strike him as nil, and things about his past that I could just as easily know simply from being his uncle. So I merely tried to comfort him while sharing in his tears. Once I'd calmed him down, we made a date for another call the next day.

I was anxious to get back home, to get back to the present. I needed to get in touch with that vast reservoir of distributed, collective memories that is the Web. But on my way home I drove past the university, right across from Papà's Faculty. The last time I'd been there was with Mamma, when I was around eighteen. We had gone, five years after the disappearance, to pick up all his books and papers. It was very depressing and even annoying. The new Dean had moved all his papers to a minuscule office without any windows. Aside from having disappeared, Papà had also been forgotten, eradicated. Maybe that was what he'd wished for. In any case, from that time on I'd never been back. But now I somehow felt like stopping for a moment. It's the middle of the summer, so no one will be there. No one at all. And nothing at all. Who knows when the anonymous flower-bearers finally stopped bringing flowers to the spot where Tessandori was killed. Now there's a plaque that says, "The State condemns and remembers . . . ," which was installed ten years after the murder. I turn around to look for the large building that had housed the library, but it's no longer there. In its place there's an enormous shopping mall, the building of which not only required the destruction of the "mass" of the library but also gobbled up the "vacuum" of all the greenery that had surrounded it.

It was a lovely day to drive around with the top down, and I felt like taking some air before returning to my attic, so I drove through the silence of the lazy, listless city, staying out until evening. When I got back home I turned on my computer, knowing that its screen would be my companion all the way to dawn. And indeed it was.

I went to Google and typed in "Tessandori." About twenty sites came up that had to do with Papà's friend. Some of them had pointers to his marvelous writings on Gropius or Mies van der Rohe, while others had links to his own projects. And then some others were dedicated to his murder. The first such site that I looked at reconstructed it in detail and additionally stated that in March of 1977 three people had been arrested, then were tried and given life sentences. Two men and one woman, just as the witnesses had reported. They had been captured in one of their hideouts. At the outset they refused to say anything, but then one of them cracked and decided to collaborate with justice. I typed their names into the search engine and out came information in greater detail. The two young men, at that time in their twenties, came from other cities, whereas the young woman had grown up on the other side of the river, where all that could be seen of the Architecture Faculty was the lush greenery surrounding its library. About this woman, Laura Giunti, there was just one short newspaper article providing a tiny bit of information. It told of a question asked by a legislator as to why a convicted murderer should enjoy the status of semi-liberty and was even allowed to work in a library. And I knew that library. And so it occurred to me that I should go seek her out. I wanted to look her straight in the eye, and perhaps speak to her.

CHAPTER SEVEN

I had bought a lawn mower—the type that has a quiet motor. That was the only feature I'd insisted on at the store. I couldn't imagine hearing any sounds in that place other than my voice as a boy, thirty years distant. The silence of that house, of that garden, had lasted for decades. And it shouldn't be broken now.

One time Uncle Giorgio—the real one—had organized a giant game of hide-and-seek in the garden. That day, my twelve-year-old cousin and the daughter of a family friend didn't scramble to get home safe and didn't come out from hiding when Uncle Giorgio gave up. People shouted their names over and over again, but they didn't answer. Finally Uncle Giorgio remembered a toolshed behind the house, at the very back of the garden. With trepidation he went back there, and in it he found them huddled together in each other's arms. Directly in front of them was a huge toad squarely eyeing them, and they seemed paralyzed by the thought that it might jump on them. Uncle Giorgio tried to liberate them by picking up a spade and shaking it while shouting. But the toad, as might be expected, leapt straight up onto the little girl's skirt, and she let out a scream that, in the silence of the garden, seemed out of place and far too loud. She tore out of the shed, still yelling at the top of her lungs, while my cousin chided my uncle, accusing him of messing everything up, as usual. And in fact, bewildered Uncle Giorgio was always doing just that.

He was actually a model uncle. He would turn up unexpectedly, bearing all sorts of gifts from mysterious worlds. He would bring books, records, T-shirts, futuristic toys, posters, drums, pennants, and every imaginable kind of doodad. He was a joyful man who loved life, and he radiated a boundless feeling of calm. He talked energetically but also knew how to listen well. He liked playing with us kids and regaling us with wild adventures that he would insist had really happened to him. He loved to catch people by surprise. Though he was a blusterer and a show-off, he was also terribly tender. When, on occasion, he did something stupid, he would put on such a glum face, like a sad clown's, that anyone who was annoyed with him couldn't keep on feeling that way. But at some point his life changed. No one ever knew why. Perhaps there wasn't any reason. He grew serious, almost sad, even tedious. The last we heard of him, he'd bought an ethnic restaurant on some island in the West Indies, and the last photo he ever sent me showed him wearing a flamboyant Hawaiian shirt. In it, he looks quite chubby, he has a melancholy smile, and he's waving at the camera.

The lawn mower held up its end of the bargain. It was quiet and efficient. And I, pushing it back and forth, turned the overgrown jungle into a quite decent lawn. Next time I'd have to get a saw to cut off all the unwanted tree limbs. But right now, Giovanni, here I am, coming straight to you. Eight-four-five-six-zero-nine-two. *Non numerantur, sed ponderantur* ("They are not counted but weighed"). These digits were winged horses, vessels flying through time, feathers that resisted the wear and tear of the decades.

"Pronto?"

Perfect—I never missed an appointment. "How's it going, Giovanni?"

"I don't know . . . And you, Uncle, when will you be back?"

"Well . . . I've still got a lot of trips coming up."

"Did you talk with Mamma today?"

"No, I only talk to you."

"How can that be? Mamma said you'd called when I was at school."

"Oh, yeah—that's true. But it was just a quick call, nothing more."

"And what did she tell you?"

"What she told me was . . . She told me that she's worried but she hopes that Papà will return very soon."

"But two full days have already gone by and we haven't heard a thing from him."

"I know. Did you ask Mamma that question we talked about?"

"Oh, yes. She told me that Papà was worried that we'd be frightened if threatening letters or phone calls were to come for him. He was very concerned not only for himself but also for Mamma and me. And so then I asked her if she thought Papà had gone away out of fear. She said she didn't know. He hadn't said a thing about his reasons on the phone, but yes, his voice had sounded frightened. And then, Uncle, I asked her another question that I hadn't dared to ask when she told me she was going to have lunch with a colleague. I asked her who it was. And she smiled at me, probably imagining some strange kind of jealousy on my part. And then she just blurted out that she wanted to talk to me as an adult—that from now on we'd have to get used to doing that. She told me once again about that evening when Papà had come back from the police interrogation and had mentioned suspicions he had about a colleague. In front of me he hadn't said the name, but he'd told it to her. It was Professor Tonini. Hearing that made me feel very weird. He's another one of Papà's friends. He's even in the photo of the housewarming of the *casa del sertão*. He's the one who's looking toward Papà and Professor Tessandori—the one in the turtleneck sweater and the jacket. Do you remember him?"

"Sure, I remember him."

"Well, Papà had told Mamma that he actually had some suspicions that troubled him—that for some time Tonini had been making strange statements. That once he'd seen him with some students who everyone knew were the most radical in the Architecture Faculty, and they were talking together in secrecy, and Papà even thought he saw them exchanging some slips of paper. And all this just a few days before the murder of Tessandori. Mamma told me that Papà had said he'd started to hang around the library more often, just to observe the movements of Tonini and those students. That was where he'd seen them together for the first time, and he knew Tonini was spending a lot of time in the library. And in fact Papà did see them there again, both Tonini and the students, but never all together. They acted like they didn't even know each other, since they didn't greet each other if their paths chanced to cross. It seemed very odd that they would ignore each other, given that he'd seen them speaking together. So Papà told the police all about it. In the next few days he learned that Tonini had been interrogated very severely at the police station. And then, ten days later, he ran into Tonini again, extremely agitated. Tonini described the interrogation to Papà and said, boiling with rage, that they'd pushed him extremely hard and bullied him, accusing him of speaking secretly with a group of students.

"So that's why Mamma wanted to see Tonini. She worked up the courage, called him up, and they agreed to meet in a café downtown. It was noisy, crowded, and filled with smoke. He looked thinner to her, and when she asked him, 'Do you know where my husband is?' he replied curtly, 'No. But even if I did, I wouldn't tell you.' Mamma was shocked and said, 'What on earth do you mean?'

'Because everyone is the captain of their own destiny. I understand your concern, but anyone who decides to run away has every right to do so.'

'Even like this, with no explanation?'

'I have no knowledge of your husband's whereabouts. Or rather, I learned after the interrogation that he was the one who had confirmed the suspicions of the police. They were familiar with my beliefs, but Professor Giacomo Astengo had told them I'd been whispering secretly with students who were suspected of terrorist leanings and that we'd had clandestine meetings in the library. That's bullshit. Or rather, I talk with whomever I want to and I say whatever I wish. That's still permitted, is it not?'"

"Mamma must have been very frightened."

"Yes, because Tonini seemed extremely upset to her. And she told me that a shudder ran up and down her spine when he said to her, 'And can you believe that when I innocently told him about the violence I'd been subjected to in the interrogations, he offered words of sympathy and solidarity! Where he is, I have no idea. For all I care, he's in hell. He can do whatever he damn well pleases. If he's running away from something or someone, that's fine by me.' Mamma took this as a veiled threat. Their drink together came to an end almost before it began, and she left. He didn't try to stop her. Mamma told me that she took a long walk all alone to try to calm down. But what do you make of all this, Uncle?"

"I really don't know, Giovanni. But I do think it's excellent that Mamma confided all these things to you. It means she thinks you're old enough not just to understand her but also to help her. Stay very close to her, please. Now *you're* the man of the house."

I bit my tongue as I said this to him, for I hated the sentiment. My grandmother had said exactly that to me one day back then, and it had deeply wounded me because it presumed that Mamma and I would remain alone. And also because it just wasn't true: I was the *child* of the house, and I had the right to keep on being just that. My father couldn't have taken away, along with his jacket with the elbow patches, my childhood as well.

"No, Uncle Giorgio. I can't handle this—I don't have the strength. I would need to know so many things that I just don't know, and so many people that I don't know. I would need to be older and I'm just not old enough yet."

I could hear some music in the background. "What's that music, Giovanni?"

"Oh, nothing. I taped *Hit Parade* off the radio and I was just listening to it. Do you know what the number one hit is?"

"No, wait. Just a minute—let me guess." Thirty years later, through a bakelite telephone, the notes of "Furia Cavallo del West" were reaching my eardrums. "It's Mal who's singing, isn't it? And what's that other song?"

"It's Daniela Goggi, singing 'O baba luba.'"

"A good year, huh?"

"So what music do you like, Uncle?"

I remained mum while frantically scouring the shelves of my musical memory for something definitely from 1977, but I came up with nothing. "The Beatles," I said, staying on the safe side.

"But they're not playing together anymore."

"Well, I just like old songs."

"Only yesterday I heard John Lennon singing 'Happy Xmas.'"

Without thinking, I blurted out, "So he's still alive?"

"Why do you ask—isn't he well?"

"Oh, I was just kidding," I replied, caught off guard. "The thing is, I haven't heard anything about him in quite a while."

"Thanks, Uncle. You help to take my mind off things. You can't imagine how empty this house feels."

"What time is it there?"

"It's morning. Mamma let me stay at home for one more day. I feel a bit guilty for having tricked her, but I just don't feel like going to school. I know she's talked with my teachers and

I don't want to see their smug looks or to have to answer certain questions. What should I say?"

"You're right. Let me think a minute. Would you do me a favor? Do you mind going out? The university's pretty close to home. Go there. No, no—go to the library instead. Tell them you're Professor Astengo's son. And get them to show you where Papà used to sit, and ask if he had a carrel where he kept his things. Tomorrow, I'll call again and you tell me what you've found out."

"All right, Uncle. Tomorrow I'll tell you."

That afternoon I went to the Ministry. There was no one there, as it was mid-August. But it was an ideal day to work, and I set about arranging all the diaries. I ordered them by author, title, and topic. I typed all the data into the computer. We have software that lets you call up items according to any label you choose. A lot of new volumes had come in. There was a teacher's diary and a country doctor's diary. A marshal in the *carabinieri* had told the story of his exploits, and a rainbow expert related his experiences. Many politicians, professors, and lawyers.

I typed in the keyword "terrorism." Just a few titles came up. Victims and murderers don't usually have much interest in writing diaries. They write essays, novels, and fictional narratives through which they convey their true stories. But not many diaries. I was struck by the title of one volume: "Of Blueprints and Blood." I didn't remember ever having read it before, so I called up the entry that described it. Its author was a woman, Patrizia Salvetti. I went to the stacks to get it.

"What are you up to? Still staying a while?" asked a co-worker who was just about to leave the deserted floor.

"Yeah, just for a little while." I'd downloaded some of my favorite music onto my computer—some famous opera arias performed on piano by Danilo Rea, and the ninth one of Elgar's *Enigma Variations*, which tugged at my heart more than any other piece. I made myself comfortable as the sun slowly set, but it was still light enough to allow me to make out the cover of the book as I started to leaf through it.

As is nearly always the case, the volume has some photos toward the middle. I flip right to them. The first one is of a child, probably from sometime in the 1940s. He's dressed in a black shirt, like a little Fascist, but he's too young for me to hate him for that. Then there's a boy in glasses who's celebrating New Year's Eve, 1955, with some friends, as the banner behind their joyous faces announces.

I skip a few photos and go to the very last ones. There's a blonde woman with large, light-colored eyes. She must be about forty or forty-five, and she's holding the hand of a young boy who's proudly displaying his soccer shirt. The picture above that shows the same woman as a little girl. I flip rapidly backwards and spot her again, now in tears, at a funeral. And then, with mounting emotion, I flip back further. There's the *casa del sertão* on the day of our housewarming. A little arrow drawn on the picture indicates Professor Tessandori. My father is right next to him, with his arm around Tessandori's shoulder. This must be a book by his daughter, and clearly she wrote it under her married name. I check it out, planning to read it tonight.

At home I find two email messages. One is from Giulia:

I'm with Stella. She can't bear having been rejected by her brother. She says he'd promised to take her to see all the places they'd seen in the movie, she says she's behaved well, hasn't done anything bad. She keeps asking for you. What should I do? Clearly I'm not enough for her. It's as if she thought it's my fault that she's "broken."

And the other is from Lorenzo:

Papà, last night, before Mamma arrived, I treated Stella to a wonderful evening. I took her to an amusement park and we went into a tunnel filled with water, hugging tightly, then we sat in one of those spinning teacups, and we went down some rapids while seated in a tree trunk. Stella laughed hard but she was scared. She clung tightly to me, very, very tightly. Every so often she would kiss my cheek and my hands. People were watching us and smiling. Then I took her to dinner in a restaurant with an Indiana Jones theme. The waiters were all dressed like Harrison Ford and they made a big fuss when they waited on us. She ate a lot and was really happy. Then we took a taxi, as she likes to do, and we went to the hilly part of San Francisco, to an area called Alta Plaza. It's full of houses with high peaked roofs and windows that bulge outward. I think they call them "bow windows" or "bay windows" or something like that. There's a playground in the park of Alta Plaza, but it was closed. So we climbed over the gate, which was very low. Stella was delighted at the thought that she was doing something forbidden. And of course she had the whole play area all to herself. She tried out all the teeter-totters, all the slides, all the animals that bounce on springs. Finally, we climbed back over the gate and sat down and looked up at the sky. It was a spectacular evening. I told her what I remembered about the Milky Way, all the things I'd studied about stars. I recalled that an exploding star can produce a supernova, and can even generate what looks like a shower of gold. Then I told her that they've calculated that there are 200 billion trillion stars. I told her something about the signs of the zodiac. And she listened to me as if I were a prophet. She was wide-eyed, with her mouth agape in amazement. She was beautiful! And I felt ashamed of myself. It occurred to me that I was doing all this out of a sense of guilt that tomorrow I'll be abandoning her. But I didn't have the courage to say a word to her about that. Only at the very end, when we stood up and were about to go get another taxi, did I tell her the truth. I told her I had

friends in Los Angeles who'd called and who needed me.
I told her that Mamma would be coming to get her and
would take her back home. "No, I don't want that. Why
can't I go with you?" I made up all sorts of explanations, but
she made each one of them sound hollow just by asking very
simple questions and reminding me of my promises to her.
"You don't want me any longer. You've grown tired of me,"
she said with a fierce sincerity.

I denied it and held her hand. Then we took a taxi back.
She didn't say a word for the whole ride; she just looked out
the window. I asked her lots of questions but she didn't
answer a single one of them. Once we were back at the hotel,
I helped her get into her pajamas. She brushed her teeth, still
wordlessly, then climbed into her bed. I turned the light off,
gave her a goodnight kiss, and went into the other room.
Then I heard her whispering, most likely so that I would
listen to her: "I wish I could be a supernova and explode
and turn into gold." I went back into her room and she
pretended to be asleep, but her eyelids were moving. I took
her hand and we both fell asleep like that.

What should I do? How often in life does one feel so split
and tormented? My rational side tells me to stay here with
her, but a different side, a more instinctive one, is pulling
me away. Or maybe it's the other way around. I'm twenty
years old and I took too much on myself. Now I'm asking you
both please to do your part.

I pretended, even to myself, not to have read either email. Instead, I just lazily clicked on Google Earth as I was reading, and zoomed in on the Alta Plaza playground in San Francisco. I found it quickly and imagined my two children there. That was the most I could do for them for the time being. My cell phone, which I'd left at home, indicated there had been a lot of calls. Demands from the world. But I, right now, have to be left all alone to read my book.

CHAPTER EIGHT

She has lovely blue eyes and long, slender hands. She's pretty, extremely pretty. She has a serene gaze and a reassuring voice. She's a grown woman with the eyes of a twelve year old. Now I'm seeing her not in black and white but in color, in the café where we agreed to meet—the same one where my mother met Professor Tonini. And when I too cross the threshold, I try to imagine where they might have been sitting and if the light was similar, since it's the same time of day.

"Signora Salvetti?"

She was looking for some papers in her purse, and on

hearing my voice she raised her head. Already she was wearing a gentle smile.

"Yes, that's me. Hello. You *are* the person I was supposed to meet, right?"

"Yes, I'm Giovanni Astengo. Please excuse me for having contacted you, but I read your whole book in one sitting and I wanted to talk about it with you."

I gave her a very quick rundown of my life, from that fateful day of March 13 all the way through the loneliness of the Ministry. I told her about my father and the diaries, and she listened to my tale without the least impatience. All around us there was a polyphony of ringing cell phones, as if they were all calling each other. Her patience was most welcome. These days, whenever you talk with someone, it's hard to get them to listen. The eyes of the person across from you often resemble black holes. Even a fool would realize that the brain, working in the back room, is only concerned with its own affairs. Most of its neurons are thinking up something brilliant that their owner can say, while others are wondering what their owner should do, purchase, or experience. Today, conversations are held in a mirror, wordless ones like the conversations in Calvino's inn, and not even helped out by tarot cards. And all the people in these desperate monologues wind up speaking only about themselves. The other party never listens, and so each party speaks just to itself and about itself. Billions of these tiny bonsai egos are wandering aimlessly about, like lost dogs without collars. Well, at least

I've made a little bit of progress: I actually *do* speak to myself, and myself replies to me as well.

But now it's Signora Patrizia Salvetti who is listening to me. Her eyes are reacting. If their movements could be captured in a graph, the emotional high points would be perfectly synchronized with the most intense moments of my strange story.

I tell her that I greatly appreciated her book, that I particularly admired the unusual serenity with which she spoke of her father's murderers. It seemed remarkable to me. So much so that it was inconceivable to someone like myself who, thirty years after the fact, is still wearing out shoes, still trudging and trudging in search of the unknown truth. She wraps her long, graceful fingers about her half-empty glass. She seems to be shielding herself from these compliments being paid to her by a stranger. After all, I've only seen her twice before—once in a televised funeral and once at a memorial service. Hardly a great way to start out, but that's how it was. Does she recall? Yes, she recalls, and she smiles. And she recalls the records of the friendship that linked our fathers. She recalls having found some notes by her father—almost a diary—of the days just after they both graduated from the university.

A diary of summer days, just like these. Our fathers took a long train trip together, heading for the sea. It's a tale of sleepless nights, of intense discussions about life and the world, about architecture and politics. They spoke of their families and of their parents. Reading that diary today conveys a feeling of serenity, like a world in springtime, filled with dreams, illusions, and hopes. Its pages record the thoughts of two youths who wanted to change the world, to change all of life—the lives of others, and of course their own. And more prosaically, they also dreamt of a Volkswagen convertible. And indeed, using the first substantial income from their joint practice, they bought one, each of them contributing half. They were happy. And then their pathways drifted apart—they started families, had children. And yet their destinies became interlinked once again in the university's Faculty of Architecture.

Patrizia (dare I call her that? I think so) remembers the *casa del sertão*. She even recalls the day of the housewarming. She's not in the photo because she'd been in a bad mood and was crying, and that would have ruined such a festive photo, marking the celebration of a beginning. But in fact her crying was an alarm call, a hint that something wasn't quite right. I speak to her about Professor Tonini. She tells me that she'd heard from her mother that our fathers often spoke of Tonini, and that her father had told her mother about some of my father's worries. But at the time, no one was dreaming that somebody might want to kill the Dean of the Faculty of Architecture. About Papà, Patrizia recalled his very touching memorial lecture a month after her father's death, and in fact she'd even mentioned it in her book. She had never forgotten the words that had concluded that speech—words written by Shakespeare, not by Professor Giacomo Astengo: ". . . and, when he shall die, / Take him and cut him out in little stars, / And he will make the face of heaven so fine / That all the world will be in love with night, / And pay no worship to the garish sun." She was moved by the image of a life splintered into a myriad of tiny stars. And for many years, as a young girl, she would press her face against her window and, just like all the world, she learned to love the night.

I had lived all my adolescent days as if they were gloomy, rainy nights. My life was defined by absence. I didn't know if my father was a hero trying to find a haven where he would be protected from assassins' bullets, or if he was a coward, a rabbit fleeing from anything and everything. Or worse yet, a walking monument to hypocrisy, someone who had simply exploited the fear endemic to those miserable years in order to forge a new life for himself. Perhaps now, in some far-off land, he was living it up in the sun, while I, day after day, was having trouble getting through the night.

Patrizia told me that as an adult she had never been able to return to the spot where her father had been murdered, but that her life had nonetheless been serene, on the whole, because she and her mother, two women, had managed to forge a delicate balance out of a network of deep and genuine bonds of solidarity. And as time passed, this network grew ever denser, finally reaching the point where it was a balm for the gaping wound created by those pistol shots. Patrizia had married, had given birth to a son—the one in the soccer shirt in the photo. And then she and her husband had separated, simply, without tensions or fights. Their life had grown boring, sad, and repetitive. There were no longer any shared joys, not a one.

And so today, at just a little over forty, she was restarting her life, which had been a series of rips, tears, and patches. And yet she had somehow managed to come to believe in the profound beauty of small things, without any exceptions. And instead of seeing life as a grand plan defined by all the standard transitions—childhood, work, marriage—she had come to see life's beauty as residing in the minute stones of an ordinary, unpretentious mosaic. She saw a smile, a handshake, a gesture, or a rediscovered scent as being worth far more than their ephemeral nature would suggest. In other words, she had arrived at the credo that life should be experienced as if by a person who constantly peers through microscopes, seeking and finding with patience and enthusiasm, rather than by merely gazing down coolly from on high, which winds up yielding only the blandest of truisms.

From this philosophy came her disarming serenity. I tell her that in the midst of horror, she had at least had the good fortune to have clarity. She knows who her father was, she knows everything about his life, she knows how he died. Whereas I've had to live with a gaping hole that was opened up by newspapers fluttering in the wind in a house that had been drained empty in the blink of an eye. And from that moment on, nothing but doubts and endless waiting. Somewhere in the world, my own flesh and blood is living tranquilly, in complete ignorance of my very existence. Or perhaps he's buried in some Buddhist or Islamic cemetery, or who knows, perhaps a Christian or Jewish one.

Together Patrizia and I formulate an idea—to publish a book, at our own expense, a book that would pull together all the writings of our fathers, most of all those concerning the architecture of chaos. They had both been deeply impressed, as Patrizia notes in her diary, by the studies of a Dutch architect, N. J. Habraken, who conceived of a freer methodology of designing and living, going as far as the idea of things that build themselves. Both our fathers had written essays on the never-built designs of Cedric Price, a marvelous visionary architect who thought of time as the fourth dimension—besides length, width, and height—of the design process. Price loved the idea that the urgency of time would change space—would have to change it. He designed buildings that played a significant role in the history of architecture, such as the Fun Palace, a multidisciplinary cultural center that he came up with in 1961. So many designs but, incredibly, only one of them was ever built—the aviary in the London Zoo, a highly symbolic structure. And, at least as legend would have it, his wife was the actress who inspired the name of the Beatles' song "Eleanor Rigby," whose refrain goes, "All the lonely people, / Where do they all come from? / All the lonely people, / Where do they all belong?"

It will be an elegant book, similar to a diary, but written by two men who no longer are alive. Thirty years later, they'll be reunited in the pages of a volume, and through it they will live again, for a fleeting instant, in the minds of those who knew them. The plan is lovely—a beautiful "architecture of time." We agree to get together again to discuss it further. Patrizia tears off the corner of a paper napkin, jots her phone number down on it, and proffers it to me. I grasp it in my hand, and she rises, lightly and gracefully. Her hair moves in a strange way. Everything seems to be happening in slow motion. Her hand grazes my shoulder and she walks by me. I don't turn. The fact that she's no longer in front of me releases my gaze. At the table next to ours is an elderly man, perhaps retired. He's sitting at an angle to the table and is nursing a coffee. He has a pad in his hands and is drawing. If I'm not mistaken, he's reproducing the counter of the café, as in Hopper's famous painting. Then he notices that I'm looking at him. He smiles at me, flips through the album, and tears out a page. He lifts it up and shows it to me, at a distance, without moving towards me. It's a portrait of me, seen through Patrizia's hair. Two large eyes, an unkempt beard, a dazed and melancholy look. And I smile back at him, but he's already gone back to staring at the counter.

The sun is setting when I get back to the country house. At this point, I've practically finished my work. The yard is presentable once more, the hedges have been trimmed, the weeds pulled out. Today I brought along a saw to prune the branches. Once I've finished that, the only thing left to deal with, symbolizing so much time gone by, will be the ivy that now covers nearly the entire visible part of the house. But I like that ivy a great deal; I'll never touch it. It's the beauty of time, the play of the sunlight, its delicate touch. This is the first time I've come here in the evening. Inside the house, everything is just the same; only the light is different. And for the first time I see light filtering through the very high old-style windows—not very much light, but amaranthine, purple, almost blue. The house seems more mysterious and disturbing. I feel no desire to stay for a long time.

"Giovanni, is that you?"

"Yes, Uncle, but why in the world did you call me at this time of day?"

"I don't know what time it is—I'm sorry."

"It's nighttime. But since I was expecting a call from you, I carried the phone into my room, with an extension cord."

"So, did you make it to the library?"

"Yes, Uncle. They were very nice and helpful. The director is a friendly woman who showed me the desk where Papà used to sit when he went there. It's right by the window that looks out onto the entrance to the Architecture Faculty. They don't have carrels for the professors. The director went off and found out which books Papà had borrowed. In them there were a few words he'd jotted down in pencil in the margins, and also a few little sheets of paper with notes written on them. All this gave the impression that Papà was expecting to return there to continue consulting those volumes. Clearly, he hadn't decided to go away. But at home, I found something else."

"What? Where?"

"I was looking through his papers on the table. In his glasses case, all folded up, there was a little piece of paper. I have it here with me. I wanted to read it to you. It says: 'Today is January 27th. This evening I saw Tonini photocopying some articles by Tessandori and me. It was late, and I was talking with a student. The School was deserted. We walked downstairs. As we passed the second floor I heard some noises. In a corner, right behind the door, there was a photocopy machine spitting out pages. I just had time to recognize one of them, an article by Tessandori that had appeared in the newspaper. There were other papers piled up on top of the machine. I was able to glimpse the cover of one of my own books. And Tonini was standing there. As soon as he saw me he came up to me, very ill at ease, and told me I shouldn't look because it was going to be a surprise for me. But he seemed too upset for that to be true. It confirmed my suspicions; for months now, Tonini seems to have changed. He's grown gloomier, he acts oddly, and he doesn't speak much. With all that's going on these days, I'll have to keep an eye on him.' And then there's one last item: 'Today, February 20th, I discovered that my desk drawer had been broken into and many papers had been taken. But the lock on the door of the professors' room is intact. Very few people have keys to it, and one of them is Tonini. I'm growing more and more worried.' You see, Uncle Giorgio, Papà was deeply frightened. Now I understand why he left so abruptly. Do you think Mamma and I should also be frightened?"

"No, no, Giovanni. Don't worry about that. What really infuriates me is Tonini's vicious behavior with Mamma. Who knows—that guy may be at the root of everything. Hang on to that little sheet of paper. Soon you'll have to give it to Mamma so that she can hand it over to the police. But I want to think of a way for you to do so that doesn't expose you all. Maybe there's some way that it could just be found somewhere, or maybe it could be sent through the mail. But I don't want you to have any more problems. Let me think about it a bit."

"Uncle, what can I tell my teachers and my friends?"

"Just tell them that Papà left on a long trip for scholarly purposes. Tell them that he went to see various works of architecture around the world, and that he'll be away for a while. Now go to sleep. We'll talk tomorrow."

"All right, Uncle. Ciao, and thanks."

The next morning I woke up to a rainy dawn. There was a strange kind of fog. You couldn't see the sky changing color, that marvelous transition. On the television, some troubling images were being shown. One was a flooded city with fires everywhere—a contradiction that the images didn't explain at all. Then there were other film clips from other places—people shouting, screaming in despair, bodies that had fallen into a river, some horrendous stampede. And then an image of thousands of shoes all in a line, like those pictures of shoes left in Auschwitz. Interrupted walks, truncated jumps, abandoned runs.

Later that morning, another Web site showed something that

restored some hope to the dawn. On the basis of long-term studies carried out at the Chandra Observatory operated by NASA, some researchers had arrived at the surprising conclusion that "a few huge stars near the gigantic black hole at the core of our galaxy were born there, despite the hostile conditions." Previously, scientists had believed that black holes always destroyed gas clouds before the clouds could condense and turn into stars.

The people who had conducted these studies were two astrophysicists—Sergei Nayakshin of the University of Leicester, in England, and Rashid Sunyaev of the Max Planck Institute in Garching, Germany. In their names and in the institutes where they carry out their research lies one of the great miracles of our day: the melting pot of diverse talents, brains, cultures, skin colors, and genes. This kind of interbreeding is becoming universal. This is the idea of globalization—the idea to which the two researchers, with their blend of different kinds of knowledge, have dedicated the days and nights of their lives, searching, investigating, and discovering the cosmos.

One of them, Nayakshin, stated, "It's quite amazing to think that a black hole could contribute to the creation of new stars, instead of just annihilating them."

And thus his words, conveyed by space-borne satellites and underground cables, finally made it all the way to my desk in this pale, colorless dawn.

CHAPTER NINE

_____

The entrance of the library is large and well maintained. When I get there, it's relatively empty. I walk into the room where you can place requests for books. There's a woman of sixty or so sitting there working at the computer. She's wearing a name tag that says "Laura Giunti." Looking at me with tired eyes, she asks, "Can I help you?" Her gray hair is pulled back and she's wearing glasses that slip down her nose. She must have been a very pretty woman.

I say to her, "Yes, I'm looking for two books: *Double Dream* by Arthur Schnitzler, and *Of Blueprints and Blood* by Patrizia Salvetti."

She looks at me distractedly and says, as she starts to consult the computer, "The first one we certainly have. I'll get it for you. I've never heard of the second one. Wait a moment and I'll check."

I wait. Several times she types in the title and author.

"I'm not finding it. What is it—nonfiction? And do you recall the publisher?"

"It's a diary and I think it was published privately."

"Oh, that's why it's not listed. We don't keep diaries that weren't published by known houses," she answers with a friendly tone.

"Why is that?" I ask her in an equally friendly fashion. "Don't true stories by real people have the right to be kept in a library? Are the only things worth keeping meditations or fictional tales? What about the struggles and pains and worries and joys and loves and hopes of simple people who've had the strength to tell others about their lives—don't those count for anything? Do only the rich, the powerful, and the famous have lives worth being preserved? Any human being has a lot to tell, you know. Even a person about whom no one else has ever written a single word."

She looks at me with surprise as she lifts her glasses off her nose. She doesn't lose her poise, remains calm and collected, seems to have been caught a little off guard, but doesn't seem upset or frightened. "Actually, I agree with you. But perhaps there are too many such diaries, and not enough room for them.

Anyway, it has nothing to do with me. What was this book about?"

"It's the diary of the daughter of a man who was killed like a dog. In the middle of the street."

Now yes—now she's upset. Her gaze darts off in other directions. She's wishing she were somewhere else. But she's right there, across from a man she doesn't know but who's alluding to things she does know.

"The author," I press further, "is named Patrizia Salvetti. However, that's her married name. Earlier, she went by another name—'Patrizia Tessandori.'"

Instead of increasing, her agitation subsides, and the look on her face turns hard and cold. "What is it that you want from me?"

"I want to tell you that I respect you for the price that you've paid, and that I have nothing against your being here, living in the world of books, something that many people would like to do. But you should read that woman's diary. Then you'd under-stand the anguish you caused. With those bullets you didn't destroy just one life. You destroyed many. Your bullet entered the body of that unlucky man, passed through it, then went around many street corners, sped through *piazze*, dashed up a staircase, knocked down doors, and wound up breaking the legs of a woman and a little girl. Then it continued further. It sailed on, unimpeded, for several more miles, entered the building where I was living, and there it broke other legs—my mother's and mine. My mother is no longer with us, and I still cannot walk, despite the fact that I've come here where you work. I merely wanted you to know this. You've paid for one murder, but they let you get away with smashing our lives and hobbling us forever."

She looks at me ever more hostilely and says, "Dear sir, you know my name. Obviously you came here to find me, and I'm not hiding from you. You see this badge? It says 'Laura Giunti.' But I haven't had the pleasure of being introduced to you."

"You're right. My name is Giovanni Astengo."

Her eyes open wide and one of her cheeks starts to quiver. She rises from her seat, walks around me, and closes the door behind us. Now I'm the one who's agitated. She motions to me to sit down and says icily, "Your account is flawed. It finishes too early. That bullet continued to wander around, unimpeded. And finally it returned to its point of origin. And it also broke *my* legs. For nearly thirty years I, too, was completely hobbled, and all I could see, in my reduced state, was the tiny space between four walls. There's no denying that that bullet came from me, and so all I can do is ask those whom it injured to pardon me. But to some degree, I too am a victim. Yes, I pulled the trigger, but do you know who loaded that gun?"

There ensues a pause, a bit too long for me. "No. Who?"

"Giacomo Astengo, the architect. Your father, I take it."

My heart skips a beat, a sudden hot flash crosses my brow, and I begin to sweat. "What does my father have to do with it?"

"Your father asked me to set up the murder of Tessandori. He was the head of our cadre, but the only one of us who had any contact with him was myself. That's how you do things when you're underground. He told me that this murder would have a major political effect, that Tessandori was a baron, that he was a big wheel at the university, and that he'd designed horrific prisons. To knock him off, so said your father, would be a lesson to many. And so I convinced two others in our cadre that this would be a just and honorable mission. One of them was an insider to the Architecture Faculty; the other one and I were outsiders. Your father helped us out with the logistical difficulties. For days on end he monitored the times when Tessandori would go in and out of the building, recording his habits. He did this from the building across the way—I think it was a library. And then he started fabricating alibis for himself. He set the date of the murder for a day when he would be giving a talk at a conference, and just to be on the safe side, he went out for lunch in a restaurant that day so that everyone could see him there. He planted suspicions on another professor—I think his name was Tonini. And then in the end your father took Tessandori's job. And that's when I realized that I'd been used. That there was no symbolic value in this murder, but simply that Tessandori was a man that your father hated and was jealous of. They'd grown up together, but Tessandori had always been better in everything. And what stung most of all was Tessandori's appointment as Dean. Clearly your father hated him, with a veiled, cold hatred. And when we were caught, he grew frightened—frightened that I would talk, that I would spill the beans. But once again he was wrong, because I never revealed a thing."

"Why didn't you talk?" I stammer.

"Because we were in love. I loved him deeply for years. That's why I never said a word. I had killed someone, but I didn't want to inflict yet more harm on other people. And so I served twenty-five years in prison. I don't know if Giacomo is alive or dead. He wounded *me*, but I did not kill *him*. As you can see, there are many of us who have been hit by that bullet. Who knows—maybe he's among them."

I couldn't keep on listening to her words. My head was spinning. I fled back to the house and bounced the sound of her sentences against the closed gate of the villa. And then, after giving the key two turns in the lock, I turned around and surveyed the garden as a whole. It was perfect—a very bright green, almost brazenly so. A piece of the present whose purpose was to keep alive a part of the past. I made a phone call and said, "Giovanni, don't worry. Your father called me. He went away for good in order to save you both. He loves you enormously but he wants your lives to go on without him. It's safer that way. You're a smart boy, and Mamma is strong. Go wherever you wish to go in life. Be curious. Care about other people. I'm telling you this because I won't be able to call you again for a while. I'm going to a country where there's no way to make international calls."

"Uncle, tell me the truth."

"Yes, Giovanni."

"Are you leaving me as well, now?" I thought I could detect his crying.

"No, that's silly. I love you. We'll talk soon."

For a short while I didn't move at all, just held the receiver in my hand. Then I took the black bakelite phone and flung it violently against the wall. I watched it break into a thousand pieces. It was as if I were watching its fragments in slow motion as they flew into every corner of the room. In that huge silence it made a huge noise. And then—nothing.

Now I understand. Now the mosaic can be pieced together again. Now everything that was churning about inside me, all shattered and jagged, has sunk to the bottom, like a flood of petals from black flowers. I don't care any longer about what I have discovered, much though it horrifies and saddens me. All that matters is that now I *do* know, that now I've seen the light. What matters is that *I* am the one who experienced all the things that took place, little by little and yet all at once, in this garden that for so many years was abandoned and overgrown, but which now has reclaimed its colors, its meaning, and its identity.

I walked outside and leaned back against the wall of the toolshed. I thought about how many lives I'd lived, about how many I would still discover and share. I thought that now I could go get Stella, and that America isn't nearly so far away these days. I thought about the fact that in my pocket I had a little slip of paper from Patrizia Salvetti with her telephone number on it, and that within its digits lay stories, lives, and possibilities. I closed my eyes and imagined being looked at by other eyes facing my own. Very close to mine, almost inside them. And I felt their separateness, their lightness. And I imagined them receding from me, slowly and silently drifting up and away. I imagined them as they rose above my face, my body, the toolshed, the villa with the climbing ivy, the garden, the neighborhood, the city, the planet, the sky, and the stars. Now I was there. I had a story to tell. And therefore, I was no longer alone.

So that's that. Now I've finished my own diary. These are the final words written about Giovanni Astengo. Now this story will be printed. Someone will read it, will summarize it, and will file it away. And thus, in this way, at long last, I will truly have lived.